One Fine Fireman

Also by Jennifer Bernard

The Fireman Who Loved Me
Hot for Fireman
Sex and the Single Fireman
(available February 2013)

One Fine Fireman

A BACHELOR FIREMEN NOVELLA

JENNIFER BERNARD

AVONIMPULSE
An Imprint of HarperCollinsPublishers

Excerpt from *The Fireman Who Loved Me* copyright © 2012 by Jennifer Bernard.

Excerpt from *Hot for Fireman* copyright © 2012 by Jennifer Bernard.

Excerpt from *Sex and the Single Fireman* copyright © 2013 by Jennifer Bernard.

Excerpt from *Three Schemes and a Scandal* copyright © 2012 by Maya Rodale.

Excerpt from *Skies of Steel* copyright © 2012 by Zoë Archer.

Excerpt from *Further Confessions of a Slightly Neurotic Hitwoman* copyright © 2012 by JB Lynn.

Excerpt from *The Second Seduction of a Lady* copyright © 2012 by Miranda Neville.

Excerpt from *To Hell and Back* copyright © 2012 by Juliana Stone.

Excerpt from *Midnight in Your Arms* copyright © 2012 by McKinley Hellenes.

Excerpt from *Seduced by a Pirate* copyright © 2012 by Eloisa James.

EPub Edition NOVEMBER 2012 ISBN: 9780062257956

Print Edition ISBN: 9780062257963

10 9 8 7 6 5 4

One Fine Fireman

Chapter One

"HERE THEY COME! Do we haf enough coffee?" Mrs. Gund called to Maribel from the Lazy Daisy grill, where she was managing twenty breakfast orders with the logistical skill of an air traffic controller.

"I'm on it!" Maribel shot a glance at the gleaming red fire engine that had just pulled up to the curb. She ran to the coffeepot and quickly filled a new filter. She ignored Mrs. Gund's grumbles, which no doubt went along familiar lines. The Bachelor Firemen of San Gabriel often showed up at this time of day, they always wanted lots of coffee, and shouldn't Maribel know all this by now?

"Order is up!"

Maribel left the coffeemaker and hurried to the opening between the grill and the counter.

"Two Lazy Morning Specials for table six." Mrs. Gund, whose tight gray curls were tucked into a hairnet, did a double take. "Maribel, vat is that you are vearing today?"

Maribel looked down at her denim overalls. They were cute, right? In a retro kind of way? "What's wrong with what I'm wearing?"

"We have da most attractive fellows in California about to valk in our door—hero firemen—and you dress like a farmer."

"I'm engaged, Mrs. Gund. It doesn't matter what I wear."

"Do not talk to me about engaged. Vat is this engaged, ven your man never even visits?" Mrs. Gund's stern face grew pink, as it always did when she warmed up to her second favorite topic, after Maribel's occasional lack of focus.

"Duncan visits, Mrs. Gund. You know he does." Maribel took hold of the two plates of Lazy Morning Specials, but her boss seemed reluctant to let them go. "And he wants to talk tonight. About something important. I'm sure it's about setting the date."

Of course, she wasn't entirely sure; she was even less sure about how she felt about that prospect.

"I tell you, he's not the man for you. How long have you vorked here, *elskling*?"

"Please. The eggs are getting cold."

"How long?"

"Six years," Maribel muttered, not liking to admit how long she'd been laboring at what wasn't even close to her dream job.

"Six years I know you. Six years dat man keep you vaiting. Meanwhile, every day these vonderful men come in here and look at you with such puppy-dog eyes, it makes me want to cry."

"You're such a softy," said Maribel, hiding a smile. Mrs. Gund, Norwegian to the core, didn't believe in giving in to her emotions, even though she had the biggest heart in the world. "I'd better take these to table six. They keep looking at their watches."

"Did you hear vat I said about the puppy-dog eyes?"

"I heard, but really, Mrs. Gund, I've never noticed anything like that. They just come in for their coffee like all the other customers."

"You don't notice? Of course you don't notice! That man has stolen your brain! He's—" Maribel yanked the plates from her grip and fled. Mrs. Gund was so silly on the topic of Duncan and her love life. The firemen didn't give her any particular looks. They smiled at everyone. They were polite and friendly and sexy and gorgeous and . . .

The door opened and three firemen walked in. Maribel nearly dropped the Lazy Morning Specials in table xix's laps. My goodness, they were like hand grenades of testosterone rolling in the door, sucking all the air out of the room. They wore dark blue T-shirts under their yellow firemen's pants, thick suspenders holding up the trousers. They walked with rolling strides, probably because of their big boots. Individually they were handsome, but collectively they were devastating.

Maribel knew most of the San Gabriel firemen by name. The brown-haired one with eyes the color of a summer day was Ryan Blake. The big, bulky guy with the intimidating muscles was called Vader. She had no idea what his real name was, but apparently the nickname Vader came from the way he loved to make spooky voices with his breathing apparatus. The third one trailed behind the others, and she couldn't make out his identity. Then Ryan took a step forward, revealing the man behind him. She sucked in a breath.

Kirk was back. For months she'd been wondering where he was and been too shy to ask. She'd worried that he'd transferred to another town or decided to chuck it all and sail around the world. She'd been half-afraid she'd never see him again. But here he was, in the flesh, just as mouthwatering as ever. Her face heated as she darted glance after glance at him, like a starving person just presented with prime rib. It was wrong, so wrong; she was engaged. But she couldn't help it. She had to see if everything about him was as she remembered.

His silvery gray-green eyes, the exact color of the sagebrush that grew in the hills around San Gabriel, hadn't changed, though he looked more tired than she remembered. His blond hair, which he'd cut drastically since she'd last seen him, picked up glints of sunshine through the plate glass wall. His face looked thinner, maybe older, a little pale. But his mouth still had that secret humorous quirk. The rest of his face usually held a serious expression, but his mouth told a different story. It was as if he hid behind a quiet mask, but his mouth had chosen to rebel. Not especially tall, he had a powerful, quiet presence and a spectacular physique under his fire-fighter gear. She noticed that, unlike the others, he wore a long-sleeved shirt.

His fellow firefighters called him Thor. She could certainly see why. He looked like her idea of a Viking god, though she imagined the God of Thunder would be more of a loudmouth. Kirk was not a big talker. He didn't say much, but when he spoke people seemed to listen.

She certainly did, even though all he'd said to her was, "Black, no sugar," and "How much are those little Christmas ornaments?" referring to the beaded angels she made for sale during the holidays. It was embarrassing how much she relived those little moments.

Tossing friendly smiles to the other customers, the three men strolled to the counter where she took the orders. They gathered around the menu board, though why they bothered, she didn't know. They always ordered the same thing. Firemen seemed to be creatures of habit. Or at least her firemen were.

Scoffing at her own silliness—"her firemen" indeed—she left table six, ignoring their pleas for extra butter, and rounded the counter. Trying to look efficient, she pulled her order pad from the pocket of her apron and plucked her pencil from behind her ear. Nervous, she used a little too much force on the pencil, and it went flying through the air like a lead-tipped missile. Kirk caught it in midflight, just before it struck Vader in the temple.

He handed the pencil back to her. Their fingers brushed. Her pulse skittered.

"Something he said?" he asked mildly.

She turned scarlet. Even her eyelids felt hot. "I'm so sorry," she gasped.

"What?" Vader asked, having missed the whole thing.

"Don't worry, Maribel," drawled Ryan. "It could

have gone in one ear and out the other and he probably wouldn't notice."

"Notice what?" An ominous frown gathered on Vader's jutting brow.

Maribel had a thing about honesty. "I almost stabbed you with my pencil. Well, not stabbed, because that's more of a deliberate thing, like *Psycho*, you know." She demonstrated with the pencil, jabbing it up and down in the air. It accidentally hit her pad and the tip broke off with a loud crack.

From behind her she heard Mrs. Gund snort. The firemen looked . . . well, she couldn't tell, because she was afraid to look at them.

"That's okay." She shoved the pad and useless pencil into her apron pocket. "I don't need to write your orders down. I know what you want."

"Are you sure?" Ryan said, a wicked twinkle in his eye. His body gave a jerk, as if one of the other firemen had shoved him. Some kind of inside joke, maybe. "I mean, let's hear it. I didn't know we were so predictable."

"Hazelnut quad shot with a Red Bull for Vader, coffee—black for Kirk, espresso with lots of sugar for Ryan—and a dozen muffins of all varieties except bran." She nodded proudly.

"Good job. High five." Ryan reached up a hand and she slapped it. Ryan was the certified dreamboat of the group, but for some reason he didn't make her feel nearly as shy as Kirk did. "How's Pete?"

"He's good. He loves the stickers you guys gave him.

He keeps bugging me about getting a ride on your fire engine."

"Open invitation. We'll roll out the red carpet for him."

She smiled delightedly, thinking how thrilled her nine-year-old son would be at the prospect of hanging out with the firemen he idolized.

"Order up," called Mrs. Gund.

"I'll have your drinks ready in a minute," she told the guys. "Be right back."

Kirk spoke, so softly she nearly missed it. "I like the new photographs." He indicated the series of three abstract shots of jacaranda trees Mrs. Gund had allowed her to display.

This time her face went pink from pure pleasure. The photographs were her attempt at art, even though they were nothing compared to Duncan's.

"Thanks." She beamed at Kirk and, as she hurried off to deliver orders, she felt as if she were floating across the scuffed linoleum of the Lazy Daisy. A single compliment on her photography could keep her going through a whole shift. Especially one from the Viking god known as Thor.

AS ALWAYS, THE teasing started as soon as they left the Lazy Daisy.

"Eight words. Anyone have eight?" Ryan climbed into the engine and picked up the onboard cell phone. "He said eight words. I had five. Anyone get closer than five?"

The sound of cheering came over the phone.

"All right, Stud, my man. Eight on the nose. Someone owes you a soda. Not me, but someone."

Kirk let the teasing roll off him as he fastened his seat belt. Let the guys joke. After what he'd been through, he couldn't get upset about a little ribbing. Besides, they had a point. Around Maribel Boone, he got tongue-tied. "They were good words," he pointed out. "She liked them."

"They were okay," said Ryan, as Vader steered Engine 1 into the stream of Monday-morning traffic. "Not the words I'd recommend. Nothing resembling, say, 'Would you like to have dinner with me?'"

"Or 'I'd like to bone the sweet bejeezus out of you,'" added Vader.

"Or 'I'm leaving San Gabriel and wanted to declare my undying love before I got on the plane,'" said Ryan.

"Or 'I'd like to lick you like a cherry Popsicle.'"

"Cherry?" Ryan objected. "Why cherry? Where do you even get that?"

"She's got red hair, is all."

Kirk finally spoke up. "It's not red. It's Titian."

Vader, not the station's most dexterous driver, turned the wheel hard as they veered around a corner. All three tilted to the side. "Titian? What's that? Some fancy word for 'tit'? I'm not talking about her boobs."

Ryan let out a hoot of laughter. Kirk shook his head. "Vader, have you ever read a book?"

"What does that have to do with Maribel's rack?"

Ryan was now laughing too hard to explain, and Kirk didn't care enough to. He'd come to blows with Vader in the past over his occasional crudeness, and it never did any good. "It's a shade of red. More like auburn."

"Huh." Since the conversation had veered away from boobs, Vader appeared to lose interest.

From the backseat, Ryan, once he'd gotten over his laughing fit, said in a lowered voice, "I'm serious, Thor. You need to talk to her. Are you going to move away without ever telling her how you feel? You've been crushing on her for years."

"I haven't been crushing."

"Right. More like drooling. I heard you muttering her name in your sleep during our Big Bear campout."

"She's engaged." It hurt like hell to say it, but he'd learned the hard way that you couldn't run from the truth.

"So you're just going to let it go? Disappear into a freakin' glacier? Seize the day, dude. Take the leap. Follow your bliss."

"One more affirmation and I'll shoot you."

"You don't have a gun. And she deserves to know." Ryan sat back with a disgusted air. "For such a tough guy, you sure are a wuss. Strong, silent type, my ass. You're afraid."

"Stay out of it, Hoagie."

Ryan shrugged. It's not like he was saying anything Kirk hadn't told himself a million times, lying awake, sick from chemo, his surgical wounds throbbing. He'd formulated the words many times. "Would you please meet me after work? I have something important to tell you." But as soon as he'd seen her today, with that delicious Titian-red hair in an unruly pile on her head, her dreamy hazel eyes widening with surprise at his compliment, the telltale color coming and going in her apple-round cheeks, he'd gone mute, as he always did.

Maribel left him speechless. Which didn't give him much of a chance to bare his heart to her.

LATER, MARIBEL BLAMED the shock of Duncan's announcement. An actual wedding date. An actual plan. One of his "friends"—a client who owed him a favor—had offered up his house in the Hamptons for a weekend. It was all too overwhelming and miraculous. She should have broken the news to Pete carefully, gently. Instead she'd burst into his room and said, with openmouthed amazement, "Duncan wants to actually get married. In July! Holy moly, Pete, it's really happening. We're moving to New York!"

Pete was sprawled on his stomach on the floor, surrounded by the drawings and notebooks that comprised his epic fantasy novel. His face had turned red and he'd yelled, "No! I hate him!"

"Pete, you don't mean that."

"I do too! I've told you a million times!"

True, he had said something of the sort, but she didn't believe he really meant it. He'd feel that way about anyone she got involved with. He wanted his mother all to himself. It was understandable.

"I shouldn't have surprised you like that. I'm sorry, Pete."

That helped a bit. The red flooded from his face, leaving behind a sea of freckles. He looked back at the giant sketchbook he'd been writing in. "You don't have to marry him, Mom. We don't need him."

"But honey, I want to marry him. We've been talking about it the last couple of years. Aren't you, you know, used to the idea by now?"

"I don't like him," Pete said sullenly. "He doesn't talk to me."

"Sure he does. When he took us to Disneyland, we talked the whole time. It was so fun, remember?"

Pete scowled at the last sentence he'd written. He had a vague memory of Disneyland, sure, but it wasn't a good one. Duncan was so fake. He'd made Pete go on the baby rides like the stupid spinning teacups. He talked only about boring things—mostly himself. He kept bragging about the famous people he'd photographed and giving Pete nasty looks when he had no idea who they were. Privately, Pete called him Dumb Duncan or, in his angrier moments, Flunkin' Duncan. If only his mother would see the truth about him.

Now his mom was giving him a "be a good boy" sort of look. "Give him a chance, that's all I ask. Can you imagine? Us in New York City! Think of all the opportunities. Museums, concerts, plays, *exhibits*. So many things to photograph, so much to see and do and eat. The best pizza in the world, Pete! We'll still be a family, you and me, with just one extra, that's all . . ."

Pete couldn't stand it another second. He leaped to his feet and ran into the bathroom, slamming the door shut.

His mother didn't follow him. One of the best things about his mom was that she knew sometimes he just needed to think. Alone.

When he heard his mother banging around in the kitchen, he skipped back to his room and flung himself on his bed. For a long time he stared at the Harry Potter posters on his wall. If only he could come up with a magic spell for getting rid of an unwanted, nasty fiancé. If only he could point his wand and say *Expelliarmus*! If only Hagrid would show up and give Duncan a pig's tail. That thought made him smile, but it lasted only a second. What was the point of dreaming impossible things? No owl was going to show up with a message luring Duncan off to the Sahara Desert. No giant motorcycle was going to blast through the air and land on top of Duncan.

A rustling sound outside made him jump. Then he went very still. It sounded as if something had landed in the camellia bushes outside his window.

The sound came again. A snuffle. A scuffling sound, like something poking at the shrubs outside.

Quietly, trying not to make a sound, Pete got to his feet. He tiptoed to the window, which was open a few inches, all his mother allowed. Slowly, carefully, he peered out. If it was a magical being, he wanted it to know he was cool with that. Whatever it was, even if it was a troll or an ogre.

It was a dog. Just a dog. A small, white dog with patches of brown and black. Bummed, he let out a long breath.

Then the dog looked up, and Pete knew, without a

doubt, that this wasn't "just a dog" at all. His mother was terribly allergic to both dogs and cats, so he'd had very little to do with them in his life. But even so, he knew this dog had to be special. He had such bright, intelligent, curious dark brown eyes, the color of the blackstrap molasses his mom gave him for iron. The dog met Pete's gaze thoughtfully, without blinking, as if any minute he was going to start talking and ask why Pete looked so miserable.

"Hey, boy," said Pete softly. "What's your name?"

The dog cocked his head to one side. He had floppy ears that looked like they'd be soft as his favorite old blankie. Pete noticed he had no collar. Did that mean he was a wild dog? Of course not. This dog couldn't be wild. He looked too nice. But where were his owners?

The dog turned and trotted off, looking over his shoulder as if asking Pete to come play. He seemed to know exactly where he was going. He moved with a tiny hitch in his stride, barely noticeable.

Pete didn't hesitate. He slipped out of his room, ran out the side door into the carport, grabbed his bike, and pedaled after the dog. He needed to call the dog something. Something special and magical. He'd call him . . . Hagrid.

Chapter Two

IN HIS DRIVEWAY, Kirk revved his Harley, listening to the odd sound he'd noticed the last few times he'd ridden home from the firehouse. Poor bike needed some work. Especially—he gritted his teeth—if he was going to sell it. Which he was. He had to. Not only did he need the money, but it would be insane to cart a Harley all the way up to Alaska so he could ride for the few months a year that had no snow. He'd considered giving the bike to his younger brother in San Diego, but everyone knew Harleys had to be earned, not gifted.

So his beloved bike would have to go. He'd been putting the moment off, but that was silly. It was just a bike. He'd take it to the shop on the edge of town for a tune-up, then post it on Craigslist or something. Unless Gonzalez, the shop owner, knew someone in the market for an older-style, lovingly maintained Harley.

He strapped on his helmet, mounted the bike, and

took off down the street. God, he'd miss this feeling, the powerful machine humming between his thighs, the wind lifting his hair, the road rising before him, chasing away every thought other than throttle, downshift, rev, signal.

Well, not *every* thought. Maribel still managed to surface, but he'd gotten used to that constant ache of longing. He didn't understand why he couldn't get her out of his mind. Sure, she was adorable, like a pink-cheeked fairy in an apron. Whenever he walked into the coffee shop, he knew instantly whether or not she was there. He could always pick up her particular scent, a light fragrance like apple blossom filtering through the thick cooking smells of grilled bacon and hazelnut coffee.

She was so creative, with her photographs and her little craftsy ornaments and beaded bracelets and such. She always had things on display at the counter, and he always bought some, whatever they were. He sent them to his family, who'd finally maxed out on the tchotchkes and suggested he share the wealth with the rest of the world. They just didn't appreciate art the way he did.

Maribel was kind too. Most of the time when he tried to buy the ornaments, she'd offer them up for free. He'd come back later and give Mrs. Gund the money. And he'd seen her with her boy, Pete. She'd sit him down at a table in the corner and help him with his homework between customers. She had a gentleness about her, something light and airy and dreamy and joyful; she'd never know how thoughts of her had sustained him during bouts of chemo.

That's why he couldn't tell her his feelings, no matter what Ryan said. He was damaged goods. A cancer survivor. How could he burden such a joyful soul with his crap? Besides, he reminded himself, she was engaged. Although the absence of her fiancé made that hard to keep in mind.

As the cheerful stucco houses of San Gabriel gave way to the grittier businesses of the industrial part of town, he kept an eye out for the cavernous warehouse where Gonzalez had set up shop. Kirk had been doing his own motorcycle maintenance for a while, but now he was under orders to stay out of the sun as much as possible. It was either build his own garage or bring the bike to Gonzalez. Just one more shift in his life.

He almost missed the big, metal-sided shop because it was lacking the huge "Gonzalez Choppers" sign with the flames around the edges. Was the G-Man making a new sign? He pulled into the big parking lot out front and knew something more was up. Usually the place had a steady flow of bikers. But now it was empty. Ominously empty. A breeze whispered through the birch woods behind the warehouse. A "For Lease" sign lay on the browning grass, as if something had knocked it over.

Was Gonzalez Choppers no more?

He knocked on the warehouse door, then realized it was unlocked. He opened it and peered inside. Yup, the place was cleared out. No jumble of Hondas, Harleys, and BMWs. No customers shooting the shit with the huge, tattooed Gonzalez. The smell was the same. Grease and diesel and leather. And a few tools were still scattered on the counter that used to be chock-full of them. Even the gumball machine that Gonzalez had stocked with mixed nuts still occupied the near corner.

When he took a step forward, his footfalls echoed in the huge, empty space. Cool air settled on his face, a relief from the typically blazing heat of a May day in San Gabriel. The only light came from small windows high on the walls. Oblique and filtered, it did little to illuminate the space. And would pose no threat to his skin.

An idea struck. Why not work on his bike here? No one was using the place, or was likely to, judging by the useless "For Lease" sign. If anyone objected, he could vacate quickly enough. He could probably make do with the tools that had been left behind. If not, he could fill the gap easily enough.

A noise caught his attention, a clanging sound as if someone had knocked something over.

"Who's there?" he called sharply.

The noise stopped with suspicious suddenness.

"Hello?" He spoke into the emptiness. "Gonzalez? Is that you?"

At his words, the sound came again, followed by a quick clicking of toenails on fast-moving paws. An animal of some kind. Kirk braced himself. There had been a few wildcat spottings in San Gabriel, not to mention packs of coyotes at night.

But the wild creature that emerged from the shadows at the back of the shop wasn't too terrifying. In fact, he recognized him right away. A little beagle. Gonzalez's beagle. What was his name again?

"Here pup," called Kirk. "I won't hurt you. What are you doing here, pup? You look like you're half-starved."

The dog's rib cage curved inwards. Poor thing must have gotten left behind. Kirk dug in his pockets for a quarter. Were mixed nuts good for dogs? Dogs ate pretty much anything, didn't they? Except chocolate.

The gumball machine dumped a handful of nuts into his palm, which he then presented to the dog. The beagle sniffed at his hand, gave him an inquiring look, then delicately nibbled at a cashew. Kirk found himself smiling. This dog had better manners than some of the guys at the firehouse. He spilled the rest of the nuts onto the cement floor so the dog could have at them.

"What the heck's your name, pup?" He remembered it had two words, and began with a *B* something. Or maybe it was a *J*. Jelly Bean? Jiffy Lube? He chuckled. "Here, Jiffy Lube."

"His name is Hagrid," said an angry young voice. Kirk jumped up and whirled around. He squinted at the figure silhouetted in the doorway. A boy, wheeling a blue bicycle through the door. Kirk relaxed.

"I don't think so," said Kirk. "I would have remembered that."

The boy came closer. Now Kirk could make out his features. A jolt of recognition shot through him, and his gut tightened. This was Pete. Maribel's kid. He quickly searched the shadows behind Pete but saw no sign of his mother.

"What are you doing out here?" he asked the boy.

"Checking on Hagrid. No one's taking care of him, so I have to."

"The guy who used to own this place must have left him behind."

"That's despicable."

Kirk couldn't argue with that. He looked down at the dog, who was finishing up the nuts. After he'd gobbled down the last one, he trotted over to Pete and sat on his haunches, licking his chops.

Pete swung a small pack off his back and dug inside it. "If you're going to give him all that salty stuff, you should give him water too." He pulled out a water bottle and a bowl. He knelt down and filled the bowl. The dog eagerly lapped at it.

"Good point. Looks like you're taking good care of . . . um, Hagrid."

Pete flashed him a pleased smile. He had his mother's coloring but had missed out on her milky skin. Instead, freckles spangled his face. Kirk ought to warn him to stay out of the sun. Instead, he asked, "Does your mother know you're here?"

Pete gave him a startled glance. "You know my mother?"

"Yeah, from the coffee shop. I'm one of the firemen who come in there."

"Oh. Cool." He seemed to be attempting an unimpressed attitude, but he didn't quite achieve it.

"So, back to my question. Does your mother know you're here?"

Pete looked down at Hagrid—fine, if it made the boy happy—and shook his head. "She doesn't know I come here, but she wouldn't care. She's too busy Skyping her dumbhead fiancé about her stupid wedding."

Ouch. Kirk felt that one like a kick in the gut. "So they're actually doing it, huh?"

"I guess." Pete shrugged.

Kirk felt for him. He recognized that helpless feeling, that knowledge that you had no control over a sudden, huge upheaval in your life. "If it makes her happy, that's a good thing, right?"

"But it—" Pete cut himself off, biting his lip. Damn, Kirk would give a lot to know what he was about to say. But getting inside information on Maribel from her kid seemed kind of low.

He also didn't like the idea of Pete being out here alone. Well, except for the dog, who might be some help if a shady character happened to wander through. Still, he couldn't, in good conscience, leave the boy alone here. Hands in his pockets, he pondered the best way to handle the situation.

"Hey, you want to help me with something?"

"What?"

"I want to see if either of these big doors are working." He indicated the two garage doors installed along one wall. "It might take two of us."

Pete jumped to his feet. "Sure. But what for?"

Kirk didn't answer. He bent to the handle at the lower edge of the door, waited for Pete to grab hold as well, then gave the signal to heave. The door resisted at first, then creaked upward with a rusty shriek. Sunlight poured in.

"It opened! But why? What do you need it open for?" Pete's sullenness had vanished in a blaze of nine-year-old curiosity.

Kirk pointed to his Harley, just visible at the edge of the lot. It glinted cobalt in the late-afternoon sun. "Work on my bike, of course."

Pete's mouth flew open. "That's yours?"

"Yep."

The kid looked from the bike to him, back and forth, over and over. Kirk didn't understand why he should be so amazed. Lots of guys had Harleys. But an expression of wonder passed over the boy's face. He must really love motorcycles. A sudden impulse took hold of Kirk. "Wanna help?"

"Can I?"

"You're here. Bike's here. Why not? As long as you call your mother first and let her know where you are."

He handed over his cell phone. Pete, with a sulky glance, dialed a number and left a grumbling message.

The next couple hours passed in peaceful male harmony. Kirk brought his bike into the warehouse, they closed the door back up, and they turned their attention to the magnificent piece of equipment that somehow brought the warehouse back to life with its presence. Hagrid the Dog dozed nearby, occasionally opening one eye to check on their progress. Kirk didn't do much; he needed more tools. But he walked Pete through the basic mechanics of the Harley. The kid ate it up. He chattered a mile a minute the entire time. He talked about his love for Harry Potter, his strong objections to soccer practice, his passionate arguments for more leniency from his mother.

Kirk wished he'd mention his mother a little more.

One thing became pretty clear. Pete really, really didn't

...ke Duncan, a celebrity photographer who had met Maribel at a gallery opening and been a pest ever since.

Kirk didn't like him either. But he liked Pete, who learned quickly, liked to laugh, and had a firecracker temper.

Neither realized how quickly time was passing until they lifted the door again and discovered night had fallen, or nearly so. The sky held deep sapphire shadows and the first twinkling of evening stars.

Pete looked stricken. "Mom's going to kill me. I'm not supposed to ride my bike after dark. Is this dark? It's not completely dark, right? Still kind of light?"

Kirk squinted at the sky. It looked pretty dark to him. "Do you have any lights on your bike?"

"No. Just a reflector."

"I'll take you home."

"What about my bike?"

"I'll bring it by later in my truck. Your mom will never know."

But Maribel was waiting on the front stoop when they roared up. A shiver of anticipation made Kirk's throat go dry. He'd never seen Maribel outside of the café. It always felt as if he was walking into some magical otherworld when they stopped by. Now here she was, on the front porch of an ordinary, rundown, suburban tract house, with the sort of stunned expression any mother would have at the sight of her son on the back of a motorcycle.

Kirk put his feet on the pavement and waited for Pete to dismount. The kid hesitated, muttering "uh-oh" under his breath.

"It's okay," Kirk called to Maribel, only then realizing he still had his helmet on. He pulled off his riding gloves and struggled with the strap, while Maribel dashed down the porch and strode toward them. Her hair swished around her shoulders, the light from the porch making it gleam like a molten waterfall. Hypnotized, he stood stock-still. He'd never seen her with her hair loose before. Sparks seemed to fly off her.

"How dare you put my son on your motorcycle? Do you know how dangerous that is? And Pete, where have you been? I called all your friends and—"

"I'm sorry, Mom!" Pete looked wretched. "Didn't you get my message at the café?"

"You know I didn't. I never get those messages. That's why you're supposed to use my cell phone."

Kirk shot Pete a sharp glance. *Crap!* He'd let the kid get away with deceiving his mother. Maribel was going to hate him now.

"I forgot. Besides, I didn't mean to stay that long. I didn't see how late it was. I'm really sorry. I didn't want to ride my bike after dark, and he offered me a ride and—"

"You're not supposed to take rides from strangers! It's like candy! Same thing! You know better, Pete."

"But he's not—"

"And you!" She whirled on Kirk again, who took a step back, holding up his hands to show he meant no harm and in the process nearly knocking over his bike. "I ought to call the police. Giving a kid a ride on a motorcycle. What were you thinking? What's next? You're going to buy him a beer? Take him club-hopping?"

"Mom!"

If Kirk could only explain, set her mind at ease, but the strap of his helmet refused to come off. He must look terrifying to her, hiding behind his helmet and black leather jacket.

"Pete, get in the house. Now." She gave Kirk one last, scathing look and turned away. His eyes swept across her pert little rear, encased in a pair of shorts, and her long, deliciously sleek legs. She was barefoot. Her feet were . . . well, kind of big and clunky. For some reason that flaw clutched at his heart. She couldn't leave. Not until he'd explained himself.

He gave the helmet strap one last yank. This time the buckle finally burst open. The helmet bounced to the ground, but he barely noticed, thanks to the pain shooting through his head and the stars dancing in his vision. Had he just punched himself in the face? He had. He felt his jaw, working it to make sure it wasn't broken. He packed a hell of a punch, if he did say so himself.

"Mom! Kirk's hurt."

"Who's Kirk?"

"Kirk! The fireman. The man with the bike."

MARIBEL FROZE, THEN slowly turned. Sure enough, the tough-looking man in the motorcycle helmet was no longer an intimidating stranger, but a wincing silver-eyed Kirk. He seemed to be weaving a little on his feet. "Sorry to scare you," he said. "Pete didn't have any lights on his bike, and it didn't seem safe for him to ride home like that. I'm a very experienced rider. There was never any danger. But I'm real sorry to worry you."

She stared. Was this really the strong, silent Kirk? She'd never heard so many words out of him at once. Maybe that bonk on the head, or whatever had happened, knocked the quiet out of him.

"Are you all right?"

"Oh, yeah. I just . . . had some trouble with my strap." He moved his jaw from side to side.

"You should put some ice on that. Why don't you come in?"

He didn't seem to grasp her meaning, gaping at her blank-faced. Poor guy must have really done a number on himself. She went to him and took his hand, which felt very warm and big. At his touch, a little sunburst seemed to light up her insides. "You'd better come in and sit down. You shouldn't get back on that bike yet. And you definitely need ice. Pete, run ahead and get a pack of frozen corn."

"Peas," Kirk said.

"What?"

Had he said something about having to pee? Unusual thing to mention. He must really be out of it. She paused and looked back at him curiously. But he was looking ahead at Pete—who had just zipped in the doorway—or maybe at her house, or maybe he was just seeing stars. Who knew? At any rate, he didn't notice that she'd stopped walking. He plowed right into her.

As she started to fall backward, he caught her by the shoulders. She clutched at his upper arms, which felt hard as rocks under his black jacket. The smell of pure, manly male—car grease and leather and open road and something else, something she couldn't quite put her finger on—went straight to her head. A liquid thrill shot through the rest of her body.

Oh my! Duncan's presence never made her light-headed like this. She inhaled a deep breath, her eyes closing partway so she could savor the scent.

"Sorry," he murmured. But he didn't look sorry. He looked . . . hungry. His head dipped lower, so she got a good, close look at his eyes. They . . . well, they smoldered, there was no other word for it. The intensity in his expression sent another shock of heat blasting through her system. She felt her lips part as she swayed toward him. What would it be like to feel his mouth on hers, taste the essence of Kirk, the power of him? She caught her breath, her lips tingling in anticipation, her body vibrating with one thought, one urge . . . and then . . .

She sneezed. Repeatedly. Helplessly.

Suddenly she realized what that other smell was, the one she couldn't quite identify.

Dog.

Chapter Three

PETE COULDN'T BELIEVE his luck. Good and bad. First there was the good luck of finding Hagrid and the warehouse he called home. Then there was the bad luck that poor Hagrid was starving, so that meant Pete had to keep riding out there and giving him food. Then the good luck of the motorcycle. A motorcycle! If that didn't prove that some magic was working—Hagrid, plus a *motorcycle*—what would? Even better luck, the motorcycle came attached to a really cool guy who let him work on the bike. Even ride it. But that was part of the terrible luck of forgetting to pay attention to the time. That wasn't luck, exactly, but still.

And now, the ultimate bad luck. His mother's sneezing fit meant that Kirk had taken off in a hurry, Pete had been plunged into a long, soapy bath, and he'd now been banned from ever going near Hagrid again.

Right. As if that would fly. Hagrid needed him.

The next day, his mother drove him to school, shooting him stern glances every couple minutes. Generally speaking, his mom was pretty cool. She was fun and listened to him and didn't get too cuddly at embarrassing moments. If not for Duncan and her dog allergy, she'd be perfect.

"I expect you at the café right after school today."

"Yes, Mom," he said dutifully. No problem. He could leave school early and ride out to feed Hagrid. Besides, his mother had a shaky concept of time. She'd never notice if he was a little late.

"Do you think he likes banana bread better or brownies?"

"Huh?" Pete was used to his mother's random changes of subject, but he couldn't follow this one.

"Kirk. The fireman." He peered up at her, noticing the pink tint of her cheeks. "I feel bad for yelling at him like that. I should apologize."

"Oh, that's okay. Kirk's cool."

"He is?" Her voice sounded odd. He didn't want her to think anything bad about Kirk, so he rushed on.

"He's the coolest guy I ever met. His favorite Harry Potter character is Hagrid too. And he thinks soccer is boring compared to rugby. He played rugby in college and broke his nose three times. And his arm. Next year I'm going to sign up for rugby."

His mother seemed to choke.

"I mean, if that's okay with you," he added hastily, remembering she had some say in the matter as well.

"Do they even have rugby for fifth graders?"

"Huh? I'll ask Kirk. He'd know. He knows a lot."

"That's funny. He's always so quiet."

Pete blinked in amazement. He and Kirk had talked the entire time they'd hung out together. Or at least, he had. He shrugged it off. "Nah, he's cool. Fun to talk to. Not like Dumbo Duncan. You would've seen if only you weren't sneezing so much."

His mom made that choking sound again. "Anyway," she said, "it's not going to come up. No more hanging out at that warehouse. No more dog. And I'll know. The nose never lies."

"Of course, Mom."

Good thing he had a plan.

WHEN PETE DIDN'T show up at the café as commanded, Maribel's already marginal efficiency vanished. She couldn't concentrate on burgers and fries when all her focus was on the street outside. Where was her little boy? And where were the firemen? If Kirk appeared, she could find out where the warehouse was and track down her son. She didn't doubt for a minute that's where he was. She'd recognized that innocent look on his face.

Finally, around five in the evening, Mrs. Gund took mercy on her and told her to leave early and go find Pete. She fled the café, jumping into her car without even bothering to take off her apron. She drove straight to San Gabriel Fire Station 1, the squat brick building in the next neighborhood over. She recognized it from the various TV reports about the Bachelor Firemen of San Gabriel.

n the street was a busy Starbucks; she wondered
vaguely why they came all the way to the Lazy Daisy for
their coffee.

She spotted Kirk's Harley in the parking lot, which
sent a wave of worry through her. If Pete was at an abandoned warehouse, she'd rather he be accompanied by
a strong, capable fireman. By the time she'd found the
side door that led into a garage filled with shiny fire engines, hurried down a long corridor lined with cell-like
bedrooms, and burst into a living-room area where firefighters were gathered around a long table littered with
official-looking pieces of paper, her heart was about to
jump out of her chest.

"Excuse me. Hello. I'm looking . . ." Her breath ran
out. She panted, desperately surveying the assembled
men. And woman.

A lovely green-eyed woman with her hair in a braid
down her back rose to her feet. "Are you okay?"

"That's Maribel. Thor's Maribel." Vader goggled at
her, as if completely discombobulated by her appearance.
"You still have your apron on."

Maribel looked down at her apron, utterly confused.
Had he said "Thor's Maribel"?

"Thor!" Ryan called. "Get out here!"

A door opened and Kirk walked out, still fastening
his belt. He stopped dead at the sight of her and said,
incredulously, "Maribel?" And then, "What's wrong? Is
Pete okay?"

Whatever progress she'd made in her attempt to catch
her breath disappeared. He was so damn sexy in his uni-

form, so fit and sturdy. But the best part was the look in his sagebrush eyes. They were wide with concern, exactly mirroring the worry in her heart. Instantly, magically, she felt less alone.

"He didn't come to the café the way he was supposed to, and I don't know where that warehouse is, and I'm sure he went there even though I told him not to, and I kind of hoped you were with him even though then I'd have to kill you both, but you're here and . . ." She stopped, gasping for breath.

Kirk stepped to her side and took her elbow. His touch was firm and infinitely reassuring. "It's okay. It's okay." He turned to a stern-faced man rising at one end of the table. Maribel recognized those remarkable charcoal eyes from the TV reports on the Bachelor Firemen. "Captain Brody, can I run her down to Highway 90?"

"That's okay," Maribel protested. "I don't mean to take you away from your job. Just tell me where it is. I can find it."

Kirk shook his head. "It's a bit out of the way. Not too easy to describe."

Captain Brody came toward them, examining Maribel closely. She nearly took a step back, but felt Kirk's hand squeeze her elbow.

"Captain, I know this isn't a fire, but don't you guys get cats down from trees and that sort of thing? There's a dog out there too, even though he probably isn't in a tree. And who knows what chemicals are at that warehouse? A fire could start . . ." She broke off, swallowing hard. Her attempt to win Brody's consent was backfiring on her, her imagination exploding with all the things that could go wrong.

"Take the plug buggy," said Captain Brody. "Kirk, you can go over the training bulletin later. And keep your phone on."

"Yes, sir."

"Thank you, thank you," said Maribel. As Kirk guided her out of the room, she asked, over her shoulder, "Do you guys like peanut butter fudge? Or I make these really cute puppets from gloves. I call them FingerBabies . . ."

"You can never go wrong with chocolate chip cookies," said Kirk, using his strong grip to navigate her past the fire engines in the garage. "But don't worry. Rescuing damsels in distress is right up our alley. We're supposed to rescue at least one a week."

"Really?" She looked up at him, noticing the curl at the corner of his mouth, the secret smile she'd always known had lurked there. It was just as endearing as she'd imagined. "Oh! You're joking."

"You sound surprised." He opened the door to a tidy red pickup truck and ushered her into the passenger seat. "Meet the plug buggy. Firehouse truck." Quickly, he jumped into the driver's seat and turned the key in the ignition.

"Well, at the café you don't say a whole lot," said Maribel, returning to the intriguing topic of Kirk's little joke. "It's mostly 'coffee, black,' and honestly, by now I know that's how you like your coffee. You don't even have to say that. But it's fine when you do," she added quickly. "I like it when you do."

He gave her a sidelong, quizzical look. Instantly her face grew warm. She pressed the back of her hand across her cheek, remembering that almost-kiss from last night. At least, she'd seen it as an almost-kiss. He probably couldn't get past the sneezing.

It occurred to her, with embarrassing timing, that she had a crush on Kirk. She went even redder.

"I guess I don't generally say a whole lot," Kirk admitted, looking uncomfortable. "But the other guys make up for it. Hard to get a word in edgewise sometimes."

"I guess that explains it. Besides, you probably say more to people who aren't waiting on you." She offered him a cheery smile. "I mean, there's not really much to say to your waitress, I suppose. Other than 'Coffee, black.' Although I do wonder why you don't mention our muffins occasionally. They're really good, you know. But you must have someone making muffins for you. Like, you know, a . . ."

"I don't," he said flatly. "No wife. No girlfriend. If that's what you're asking."

"Really?" If her face were any more red, she'd be a strawberry. Of course she'd been asking him that—in the clumsiest possible way.

They drove over a pothole. She bumped against him as they landed. Her arm tingled even though she hadn't actually touched his skin. "But you're so . . . you must have girls . . . is it the Bachelor Curse?" Rumor had it the San Gabriel firehouse was cursed, so its inordinately handsome crew had a rough time in the romance department.

A smile touched his lips. She wanted to touch them too. Very badly.

"Don't know about that," he said. "It's more of a . . . well . . . it's hard to explain."

"That's fine. You don't have to." Despite herself, disappointment swamped her. She really wanted to know Kirk better. Something lurked behind that silent exterior, something intriguing. But it was hard to pry information out of him. Kind of the opposite of Duncan, who could fill an entire long weekend with anecdotes about photo shoots with Christina Aguilera. "We can stick to 'coffee, black.'" She gazed out the window, trying not to feel hurt. She was being ridiculous anyway. What did a motorcycle-riding fireman and a wannabe-photographer waitress have in common?

KIRK GRIPPED THE steering wheel until his knuckles turned white. He'd offended her somehow. Her lovely face had gone closed and stiff. She was no longer chattering about muffins and girlfriends. She propped her elbow on the car door and rested her head on her hand. Her red hair glowed ruby in the twilight, the last rays of the sun turning her skin a vibrant gold. He couldn't believe she was sitting right next to him, like a fantasy come to life, even down to the apron that occasionally turned up in his nighttime yearnings.

What had he said wrong, and how could he fix it? They'd almost reached Highway 90. Shortly they'd arrive at the warehouse and the moment would be gone. Just like the guys said, he should tell her the real reason he went so tongue-tied in her presence. The reason he stuck to "coffee, black" and was damn proud he got that out. If he didn't say anything, she'd continue to think he didn't care to converse with her, or that he saw her only as a food deliverer and nothing more.

"It's not that," he said through gritted teeth. "It's more like . . . a sort of situation." He winced. A situation? What the hell?

She looked confused. "What kind of situation?"

"*Situation*'s the wrong word. More of a . . . reaction. A strong reaction. When I . . . well . . ." Damn, this was hard. How could he possibly explain that he'd tried dating other women but kept thinking about her, and that he tended to go mute and awkward in her presence? But that was just part of the story. The rest of it . . . he couldn't tell her that either, she might feel sorry for him or see him as weak. But the expression on her face—wary, trembling on the edge of hurt—reeled him in like a hooked flounder.

"I had skin cancer," he blurted. "Stage Three."

She whirled in his direction. "What?"

Oh lord, now he'd made everything worse. He should have just told her he had a crush on her. No going back now. "I *have* skin cancer," he corrected himself. "I went through treatment. It might be gone. But there's always a chance it could come back."

"Skin cancer," she repeated softly. "Is that why you were gone? You didn't come to the café for a while."

The fact that she'd noticed his absence made him want to crow like a strutting rooster. He tamped down that entirely inappropriate reaction. "Yes. I couldn't work when I was on chemo. I wanted to, but I couldn't. But I'm back now." Not for long, but he didn't want to tell her that. At least not yet.

She put her hand on his forearm. His muscles tensed at her touch. He wanted to look at her, see how she was reacting to his revelation, but instead he stared at the road ahead. Only a few miles to Gonzalez's now. *Way to ruin the mood, asshole*, he lectured himself.

"I'm so glad you're okay now. I wish I'd known. I would have sent you a card or visited you in the hospital." A card. If she had any idea how many times he would have read anything she sent him. She could send her electric bill and he'd pore over it looking for doodles.

"That's okay. I wouldn't want you to worry. Or anyone else. That's why . . ."

"That's why you don't have a girlfriend," she finished for him. "Because you wouldn't want her worrying about you?"

"Right. But more than that. I wouldn't want to make things hard on her. You can't be much of a partner if you're sick all the time."

Maribel was shaking her head back and forth. Every time she did so, another strand of tempting Titian silk strayed from her ponytail. His fingers itched to tuck them back behind her ears. "But that's so wrong."

"I don't want anyone's life complicated because of me. The guys at the firehouse were great. They really came through for me. But the girl I was sort of dating, well, it didn't work out."

"She must not have really loved you."

Hearing the word "love" from her mouth gave him a bittersweet shock. If *she* loved him, he'd be able to lift apartment buildings with one hand, jump to the moon, swim to the stars. But she was engaged. And thought of him as a taciturn occasional customer.

"I'm a firefighter. I watch out for people. Rescue damsels in distress." He tried for a wink, though it came out more as a grimace. "Not the other way around."

"Kirk! You have it all wrong." Her forceful tone gave him a start. "Just look at me."

He took that as an invitation to stare at her, even though she clearly meant it metaphorically. "I'm looking."

"I mean, look at me freaking out about Pete. I'm worried, right?"

"Yes, but you shouldn't be. He's okay, especially if he's with Hagrid. That dog's a lot tougher than he looks. I hung out there working on my motorcycle and no one showed up all day. Just Pete, me, and Hagrid. Believe me, I won't let anything happen to Pete. We'll be there in a couple of minutes and you'll see."

He turned onto the winding road that led to the warehouse.

"That's not the point!" She bounced on the seat in frustration. "I'm worried, but I don't *mind* being worried. I mean, I mind to the extent that I'm going to be pretty darn pissed at that kid and he's going to know it. Consequence city."

"Give him a break. He really cares about that dog."

"Forget the darn dog!" Surprised by her intensity,

Kirk screeched to a halt outside the warehouse. Pete's blue Schwinn was right where it always was, and he heard Hagrid bark from inside the building. "It's not the end of the world to worry about someone. I'd rather have someone to worry about than never worry again. If you want to worry about something, worry about why you don't have anyone to worry about you! Except now you do."

"What?"

"Me, you goof. I'm going to worry about you no matter what you say. I don't care if you're a big strong fireman who rescues people with his bare hands. Why should that mean you don't deserve someone to worry about you? Well, you do. And I do. So there."

With an emphatic nod of her head, she hopped out of the plug buggy. Kirk rubbed the back of his neck. That conversation was going to take a lot of sorting through. Later, after they'd found Pete. But for now, he kept hearing those two words, "I do," echo through his brain.

God, he was such a hopeless fool.

Chapter Four

THE SIGHT OF Pete's bike both reassured and infuriated Maribel. So her son had ridden out here in direct defiance of her orders. Maybe Duncan was right and she was too lax, too easy on Pete. Once they got married, would Duncan get more involved in disciplining Pete? They'd never discussed that sort of thing. Pete wouldn't like that much.

Then again, right now she could use a little help in the discipline department. She flung open the door to the warehouse and peered into the dim interior. A sharp flurry of barks greeted her. Something warm kept bumping against her shins, but she couldn't make out anything in the darkness.

"Pete!" she yelled in a panicked voice.

"Down, Hagrid!" came her son's voice. "Down. Be cool." *Hagrid?* Maribel peered at the creature at her feet. As her eyes adjusted, she realized it was a dog. A pretty darn cute dog. Mostly white, but he looked as if someone had spilled black and brown paint on him. He stared up at her with melting brown eyes. She took a step back and collided with Kirk. He put his hands on her upper arms and gently moved her aside so he could step in front of her.

"Come on, boy." The dog, following the firm command in Kirk's voice, trotted after him. "Pete, tie him up. You know your mom's allergic."

Right on cue, Maribel sneezed. Her eyes itched. She blinked madly, blurring the sight of the stubborn scowl on Pete's face. He bent down to snap a rope on the dog's collar. The other end of the rope was tied around a post. He petted the dog, murmuring to it.

Maribel felt like Cruella De Vil. Still, she had to take a stand. "Pete. I told you to stay away from this place. It's not safe. It's an abandoned warehouse, for goodness' sake."

"It's not abandoned. Kirk hangs out here. So does Hagrid. Just because you're allergic doesn't mean I should never get to have a dog. And I don't even *have* Hagrid. I just get to visit him. And now I can't even do that. It's so unfair!"

Oh Lordy. If he'd named the dog Hagrid, the chances of a peaceful resolution to this mess were zero. She cast a helpless glance at Kirk.

"The dog belonged to the guy who used to rent this place," he explained. "He had a motorcycle shop here. Looks like he left his dog behind."

"That's terrible."

Pete's face brightened. Maribel tried to steel her heart against all sympathy for the dog.

"Pete found him, and he's been taking good care of him. Pete says he's actually put on a little weight."

"When I got here, he was sleeping and I thought he might be sick. I didn't want to leave him all alone. Look, I taught him a trick."

He gave Hagrid an elaborate, spiraling hand signal. Hagrid, with what looked distinctly like a sigh, rolled over quickly, then popped back to his feet again.

Kirk laughed, which made Maribel glance at him in surprise. She'd never seen him look carefree before. He always seemed so serious, even when ordering coffee. "Hagrid's a smart dog. He used to ride with Gonzalez sometimes. The shop owner. He sat in front, even had a helmet. Cutest thing you ever saw."

Maribel shook her head in despair, then sneezed again. "Pete, what do you want me to do? We can't bring the dog home. You know we can't."

"Because we're moving to New York?"

Maribel felt Kirk glance sharply in her direction. Her face went warm. Should she have told Kirk they were leaving? But they didn't know each other that well yet. "That's not why and you know it."

Pete bent to cuddle the dog again. As he scratched between Hagrid's floppy ears, the dog's tail thumped the floor. "Then why can't I just keep doing this for now? Take care of him out here? He likes this place. So do I. It's fun."

"Because . . ." Maribel put a hand to her forehead. Was she in the wrong here? Where was the section in the nonexistent motherhood manual that covered this situation? What would Pete's father say? Then again, his father, having left town and changed his cell number the instant two lines appeared on the pregnancy test, probably wouldn't be the best guide. "Because it's an abandoned building. If I let you play here unsupervised, they'd take away my Mom card."

"There's no such thing as a Mom card."

"I'm sorry, Pete. It's just not safe." She took a deep breath. "I think we should take Hagrid to the animal shelter so they can find him a good home."

"*What?* They kill dogs there. You know they do!"

Maribel winced. Wrong move. "We won't let that happen. We'll keep checking in. If no one adopts him, we'll find someone ourselves."

"But we don't know who's going to adopt him! It could be someone horrible who never takes him for walks and feeds him crappy food and doesn't care about him!"

"Pete, be reasonable."

Pete screamed at the top of his lungs. "*You're not being reasonable! You're being horrible! You should . . . they should . . . take away your Mom card!*"

Maribel felt the warehouse shift around her. She thought Pete had outgrown his terrible tantrum phase. His outbursts could be horrible. Nothing made her feel worse or more incompetent as a mother. And Kirk was about to witness the whole thing, see how inept a parent she was, how little control she had over her son, how . . .

She felt a hand drop to her shoulder, a strong, warm hand. Kirk's calm voice carried through the charged atmosphere like headlights through fog.

"Your mom's right, Pete. I'd never have been able to play alone out here when I was a kid. I'd have been grounded about ten times over by now."

Pete gave a surprised hiccup. Had Kirk managed to stop the hurricane before it truly got going?

"But I do have an idea. Pete, can you give us a minute? I'll run it by your mom first and see what she says." Not giving Pete a chance to answer, he took Maribel by the elbow and led her outside into the bright air.

"I'm sorry about that," she mumbled, mortified. "He can be pretty fierce sometimes."

Kirk shrugged, as if it was no big deal. "I was wondering how you would feel about Pete coming to feed Hagrid if I'm with him."

"You mean . . ." She frowned. "You'd bring him out here? Every day?"

"Not every day. Can't when I'm on shift. But most days I could. I'm working on my bike here anyway. It's no trouble."

"No trouble?" She looked at him skeptically. "You're basically offering to babysit my kid and his stray dog. Don't you have other things you'd rather do?"

A funny look crossed his face. He opened his mouth, then shut it again quickly.

"Anyway," she continued, "it's not a long-term solution. He'll just get more attached to the dog and . . . I don't know anything about that dog. What if he has rabies or fleas or mad cow disease or . . ."

Kirk seemed to bite back a laugh. "I can vouch for Hagrid. Gonzalez always took good care of him. But I'll take him to a vet and get him checked out."

"But . . . we're going to be moving and . . ." She swallowed. Strange how hollow that last statement made her feel.

Kirk didn't seem to like the sound of it any better than she did, judging by the way his body stilled. "Pete and I will work on finding a home for Hagrid. Someone Pete likes. I'd take him, but . . ." He snapped his mouth shut, as if he'd nearly said too much.

"You mean, you'd help him with the transition to a new owner."

"Yeah, I guess."

"Transitions are hard on kids," she explained. "That's what all the parenting books say."

His silvery eyes looked down on her with such sympathy, she found herself spilling out more confidences. "I read a lot of parenting books. My parents weren't . . . well, they travel a lot. All over the world. Everywhere except here. The air's bad here." Yes, that sounded just as lame is it had when her mother explained it to her.

After a moment, Kirk asked, quietly, "What about Pete's father?"

Her eyes flicked away from his and focused on the chest muscles under his dark blue SGFD shirt.

"Pete's never met him. I know it must be hard. That's why I want some stability for him. A male figure in his life. Duncan thinks Pete needs a stronger hand. He's probably right. Pete used to have these tantrums . . ."

Even though she was still concentrating on his broad chest, she caught a glimpse of his jaw tightening. A muscle flexed in his neck. It was fascinating, watching these little signs of his inner thoughts.

"I don't know about that," he finally said, as though he were restraining himself from saying something much different.

"Know about what?"

"Pete's a good kid. You see a lot of kids in my line of work. There's nothing wrong with your son."

As much as Maribel wanted to believe that, she couldn't help giving him a skeptical frown. "But you aren't a father, are you?"

"No. Is Duncan?"

Good lord, was that jealousy in his voice? And what was that hard look in his gray-green eyes, as though the next celebrity photographer he spotted would go flying across the room in a bloody blur?

Something inside her thrilled to the restrained force etched in every line of his body. What would it be like to feel that strength against her . . . inside her? She shivered.

"Mom? Kirk?" Pete called from inside the warehouse. "What are you doing?"

What *were* they doing? Kirk stared down at her with a look that screamed possessiveness. And she . . . she was gazing back, lips parted, breath coming quickly . . . Were they suddenly standing closer to each other than they had been two minutes ago? She didn't recall stepping forward, or seeing him do so. And yet, her skin was tingling at his nearness, the little hairs on her arms were standing on end, as were her nipples . . .

Good Lord almighty, this had to stop! She took a wild

step backward, only to feel Kirk's hand catch her before she tripped over a chunk of concrete.

"See?" she said triumphantly, waving a finger at him. "Pete could stub his toe on something like that. He could fall on his face, start bleeding, get a concussion, not be able to find his way home . . ."

The confusion in his silver-lit eyes brought her back to earth.

"Ugh, there I go, catastrophizing again. Bad habit."

He just kept looking at her as if she were the most fascinating being on the planet. "What's that?"

"Think of the worst possible thing. All possible worst possible things. I do it a lot, ever since I became a parent."

"It's good to prepare for the worst. We do it when we fight fires too."

"Yeah, but I think I might go overboard sometimes. It's hard to say. It's not like they have a catastrophe chart in any of the parenting books."

Amusement lit his quiet face, transforming it from handsome to dazzling. A dimple appeared in his cheek, erasing his tired, drawn look. "I think you're doing great, Maribel. You don't need to worry so much."

Pleasure flooded her, chasing away the thought that Duncan said pretty much the opposite.

"*Mom!*"

"Fine," she said quickly, knowing from the impatient tone in Pete's voice exactly how much time they had left. "You can bring Pete out here to take care of Hagrid. But you have to be with him the whole time. And if he has schoolwork or soccer practice, that comes first."

"That's fair."

"And you promise you'll help him find Hagrid a good home?"

"Promise."

At his solemn tone, that of someone taking a sacred vow, she felt an unstoppable urge to thank him. Before she knew it, she was teetering forward, rising on tiptoe, and touching her lips to his jaw. The slight roughness of his past-five o'clock stubble tickled her mouth. The sunny, open-road scent of his warm skin went right to her head. His head started to move, his mouth coming toward hers, she could feel his hot, intoxicating breath against her cheek, she swayed toward him, wanting him, wanting all of him, but for now this would do, just the feel of his mouth against hers . . .

A brief, scalding contact sent fire racing through her veins. *Holy crap*, she thought wildly, before feeling his body pull away from hers, his lips lift away from her mouth. The door was flung open and Pete stared at them like an indignant, red-headed avenging angel.

"I've been yelling and yelling in there. Are you both deaf?"

"We've been working something out for you, Pete," said Kirk calmly, though his eyes had darkened and his chest rose and fell more quickly than normal. "I'll be your Hagrid-feeding escort. Every other day or so, we'll come out here and bring him some more food, play with him and so forth."

"Every *other* day?"

"I gotta work. You know, putting out fires, saving

lives." A smile ghosted across his lips. The lips that had just been touching hers, that had kissed her with a kind of intensity she'd never imagined from quiet Kirk. She put a hand to her mouth.

"I guess that's okay," said Pete.

Maribel made a mighty effort to get a grip on her unruly reaction to the sexy fireman. "Pete, Kirk will be in charge. He's doing a really nice thing for you, and I want you to appreciate it."

"I do. I do. Thank you." Pete bobbed his head fervently.

"And your schoolwork comes first."

"Sure."

"No schoolwork, no Hagrid," she repeated, just to drive home the point.

"Mom, I get it."

"And you're grounded for two days because you disobeyed the rules and came out here today."

He groaned. "Fine."

She dared a glance at Kirk, almost afraid she'd burst into flames of lust if she looked directly at him.

He was nodding gravely. "Very fair."

"Grrrr." Pete whirled around and disappeared back inside the warehouse, leaving Maribel and Kirk staring at each other awkwardly.

"I . . . I'm sorry," he muttered. "I know you're engaged, and I shouldn't have done that."

Her jaw dropped. Horror-struck, she stared at him. *Engaged.* Good lord, she'd forgotten all about Duncan. Not just during the kiss, but after, all the way until he'd brought it up. If he hadn't, when *would* she have remembered? Sometime before the wedding, she hoped.

She stammered something and spun around to go after Pete. This wasn't good. Not good at all.

As soon as she'd put Pete to bed, she called Duncan. Good thing he kept rock-and-roll hours to match those of his clients. "Duncan, you have to come visit. Really."

"Why, baby? This is a busy month, you know. I have three shoots in the next two weeks."

"But Pete needs to get to know you better." She landed on the first mentionable reason she could think of. "He's freaking out about us getting married. I was thinking some time alone with him would be good."

If it worked for Kirk, why not Duncan? Logically it made a certain amount of sense, even though she had a sneaking suspicion it wouldn't be the same at all.

"Time alone? If I'm coming all the way out there, I want time alone with my babycakes."

"Well, of course, that too." That was the main point, wasn't it? To get Kirk out of her brain and Duncan back into it? "I miss you."

"I miss you too, Mari. But just think, before long we'll be together all the time. Can't wait, baby!"

"Me neither. So you'll come?"

"Let me check my schedule . . ." He put her on speaker so he could pull up his calendar. "Yes, let's do it. Maybe I can set up some meetings while I'm out there. You wouldn't mind a road trip to LA, would you? I could take you to Bar Marmont. Bet Pete would like that. Maybe I can wrangle a run-in with Daniel Radcliffe."

Now that, Maribel had to admit, would actually impress Pete, though he normally scoffed at all of Duncan's celebrity references. When she hung up, she felt a little better. Duncan loved her, surely he did. He could have any number of high-profile girlfriends. And he had, before he'd met her. He'd even dated a Victoria's Secret model and one of Madonna's dancers. But he claimed Maribel was perfect for him, his haven from the fame-hungry world in which he lived.

Yes, Duncan loved her . . . and respected her, right? Sure, he laughed a little at her reverence for the "art" of photography. Not that she claimed to be an artist, of course, but she had an awestruck admiration for those who were. Duncan found it adorable in the same way he found her photographs adorable. But that was good, right? She didn't need him to think she was a genius. As long as he respected her, which he did, didn't he?

Anyway, he'd finally picked a date, they were getting married, and that was that. Pete would grow to appreciate Duncan's good qualities, as well as the amazing Manhattan lifestyle they were about to adopt—think of the schools, the museums, the culture—and he'd forget all about a goofy dog named Hagrid and the kind, pulse-poundingly handsome fireman he'd befriended.

Uninvited, thoughts of Kirk came flooding back. Not just the kiss, but everything he'd told her in the plug buggy. His bout with cancer. His refusal to be a burden on a girlfriend. Maybe he thought that was heroic, but it made her angry all over again. Damn it, someone like Kirk, someone strong and thoughtful, someone who spent his life watching out for other people, running into fires, helping out little boys, taking care of abandoned dogs ... someone like Kirk ought to have a woman standing by him. Babying him. Loving him. Making love to him ...

She groaned and went to take a shower. Duncan better get here soon.

Chapter Five

KIRK'S ONLY QUESTION about what had happened at the warehouse was: How badly had he screwed up? Maribel had snagged Pete and run out of there so fast, he'd barely had a chance to scribble his number on a piece of paper and hand it to the kid. But maybe the deal was off now anyway; no phone call so far, and it had been two days.

Worried about Hagrid, he'd gone out to the warehouse alone with a can of Science Diet, tossed a stick for the pup until they both got bored, then scratched his ears and said goodbye.

But not before he'd shared a few secrets with the dog, who made a comfortable, floppy-eared confidant. "She liked that kiss as much as I did, you know. And she kissed me first. Sure, it was a little peck on the jaw, but when she put her lips on me, I couldn't think straight anymore. Can you blame me? Well, *she* might blame me. Then again, I think she was mad at herself more than me. She's not the type of woman who would cheat on her fiancé. She's probably beating herself up. Catastrophizing." He smiled at Hagrid, who cocked his head, apparently following the one-sided conversation perfectly well. Or else wondering when Kirk would break out the next snack.

"I'm just not sure what to do next. Ryan would probably say, 'Ask her to dinner.' But that would make it worse, wouldn't it? Then she might think that I thought she was the type of woman who would two-time her fiancé. You know what I mean?"

Hagrid laid his head on his paws. Kirk stroked his soft ears until his tail thumped happily.

"It's tricky. And it makes it worse that it's her. Because I don't want to make a wrong move. Freak her out. Even more than she already is, I mean. Damn. Maybe I'll see what the guys think."

Even Hagrid seemed to think that was a terrible idea, judging by the snuffling noise he made as Kirk scratched the notch between his shoulder blades.

"I know. Bad idea. Not happening anyway."

What could he do, besides hope that Pete would give him a call soon? He surged to his feet, so frustrated he tossed the empty tin of dog food in the garbage can with enough force to make it ring like a bell of doom. God, how pathetic could a man get, waiting for a call from a nine-year-old boy? Why had he made that offer anyway? All it guaranteed was time with Pete, not Maribel. He felt like a man wandering the streets, pressing his face against the window of a cozy home for a glimpse of the happiness inside.

Pete was going to be someone else's stepson. Maribel was going to be someone else's wife. He was going to move to freaking Alaska. And Hagrid? He'd make a few calls, see what he could drum up.

In the meantime it would probably be best for them all if his number got irretrievably lost in the chaotic jumble that lived inside Pete's pockets.

BUT IT DIDN'T. The next day, Maribel called. Actually, the next evening. Kirk was playing pool when his cell phone rang and ruined his bank shot into the corner pocket.

"Yeah," he answered abruptly, not bothering to check the number.

"Is this Kirk?" The sound of her soft voice made him straighten up, knocking the chalk off the side of the table.

"Yes. Sorry." He swung around so the guys couldn't hear him. "Maribel?"

"Wow! Good guess."

Right. As if he wouldn't know her voice anywhere.

"I . . . uh . . . have kind of a strange favor to ask. My babysitter canceled and I've been calling around everywhere, but no luck. Pete came up with the idea of hanging out with you tonight. I told him you were probably already busy, or else working, but I promised him I'd check. So this is me, checking. Please don't be offended that I even asked; it was Pete's idea and he gave me your number, and . . ."

"Sure."

"Really?" The delight in her voice sent blood rushing to his head. "You're free?"

"Well, I'll be home soon. Say, ten minutes?"

"Oh my God, you're a lifesaver. I can . . . maybe I can bring you some cookies or something? Fudge brownies?"

"Don't worry about that. You can set me up with some more ornaments next Christmas, how's that?" Kirk winced. His family would stage a revolt if any more ornaments came their way. He'd have to find a worthy charity.

"Done! For the next five Christmases, if you like. I always have a lot left over."

Kirk gave her his address, then handed off his pool cue to Vader. Of course nothing was that easy; as soon as he explained, the teasing followed him right out the door.

"Thor, you wuss. Who are you, Mary Poppins?" Ryan winked. "Bet you're after that spoonful of sugar."

"Adventures in babysitting, dude. Adventures in babysitting," said Vader cryptically.

"My sister watched that movie about a hundred times," said Fred the Stud with deep nostalgia.

"I saw that one," said Ryan. "Elizabeth Shue was cute in it. Damn, I just remembered . . . the bratty kid in that movie liked Thor. Wore a helmet and everything."

"Thor the Babysitter. Never thought I'd see the day." Vader shook his head.

Kirk managed to escape without bloodying anyone's nose, which he considered a personal triumph. He cruised home on his bike, barely making it ahead of the battered old Volvo containing Maribel and Pete.

The thrill of Maribel at his front door, of his porch

light striking copper starbursts in her glorious hair, of her apple-blossom fragrance drifting inside his living room, gave him a high that ended only when Pete explained, gloomily, that Duncan was in town and Maribel wanted some time alone with him.

At that point, Kirk figured he deserved every scrap of ribbing the guys could dish out—and then some.

MARIBEL RUSHED HOME, where Duncan was still finishing up a phone call. He didn't even look up when she burst into the house. "Ready!"

"Who'd you find?" Duncan asked vaguely, though Maribel knew he didn't really care and wouldn't remember the answer if she told him. Maybe the news that a handsome fireman was looking after Pete would make him sit up and take notice, but probably not. If Duncan was jealous of other men, he'd never shown it during six years of a long-distance relationship.

"Just a friend." A friend who'd kissed the sense out of her, but no need to go there.

Their dinner date was not what Maribel had hoped for. Duncan's phone call had put him in a bad mood. Maribel knew the signs. Prolonged silences, preoccupied glances, sudden bursts of animated ranting. Moments of great charm directed at the waitresses alternating with sullen monologues about why the West Coast scene was entirely inferior to New York's. There was no point in debate; Maribel knew her role. Listen sympathetically, offer unquestioning support, be the haven he saw her as.

The thing was, she didn't feel like a "haven." She had things on her mind. Pete, for one. When Duncan's flow of complaints seemed to be easing, she grabbed the opportunity. "Have you thought about what you want to do with Pete while you're here?"

"Huh?" He looked at her blankly, almost as if he'd forgotten she knew how to speak.

"You know, some Pete-and-Duncan alone time. To give you two a chance to bond."

"Oh." He waved his fork, on which perched a chunk of baked Brie. "I don't think that's going to happen this trip, baby. Next time."

"What? Why not?"

"Haven't you been listening? The Chicksie Dicks are freaking out. They want a reshoot."

The Chicksie Dicks? That didn't sound right. She really had been zoning out while Duncan vented. She wanted to ask if the Chicksie Dicks were a real group or if he was making fun of the Dixie Chicks, but now she didn't dare. He'd never forgive her if he knew she didn't hang on his every word.

"But Duncan, you keep talking about being Pete's stepfather. You want us to be a family."

"Of course I do."

"Shouldn't you get to know him better?"

"What's to know? He's a nine-year-old boy. I was nine once. I know what it was like. It sucked. If someone had come along and offered me backstage passes to the Beastie Boys, I'd have been his slave for life."

"But Pete's not that into music. He likes to read. He's

got a great imagination. You should hear some of the things he makes up. He's convinced an owl will show up when he's eleven with an invitation to Hogwarts. He's even written his own novel—well, started it. But he's two chapters in and it's fantastic . . ."

But Duncan's phone had buzzed; a text had come in. He immediately began scrolling through the message and cursing. Maribel wanted to scream with frustration. His distraction had never bothered her until now. It hadn't really mattered because their lives were so separate. But if they really were going to become a family, it did matter. She couldn't let this slide. She waited until he finished his reply text, watching the top of his sandy brown head as he hunched over his phone. Duncan was good-looking in a bland, prep-school sort of way. He'd grown up in the sub-urbs of New Jersey with the sole dream of breaking into the Manhattan hip crowd. He'd done it too, and wore the black jeans and horn-rimmed glasses to prove it.

She'd assumed the fact that he'd chosen her, someone with no social connections or any kind of status in his world, meant he wasn't really the snob he appeared to be. But was that really true? Why did he want her?

"Duncan," she said, when he'd finished his text. "Why do you think we should get married? I mean, things are good the way they are, right? We do okay, for a long-distance relationship. We're both busy with our careers. I've got Pete, you don't really want more kids." This gave her a secret pang. Pete would love a sibling. She forged ahead. "Why mess with a good thing?"

Duncan dragged his gaze from his phone. "What?"

"Did you hear any of that? Do I need to repeat the whole thing?"

"Sorry, baby. You know how it is." God, his phone seemed to have a gravitational pull stronger than Jupiter's. It was winning again; she was losing his attention.

She kept it short and sweet this time. "Why do you want to get married?"

"What?" He frowned behind his horn-rims. "I told you. Because you're my haven."

"Okay, but . . . do you think you could elaborate just a little? How am I a haven?" And how was that not like being compared to a retirement home? *Ooooh*. She drew in a breath. Was that it? Did Duncan see being with her as the equivalent of an emotional retirement from the Manhattan dating scene?

"It means"—he shot an angry glance at his phone, where apparently things were not going well—"you're not needy and demanding. You let me do my thing without wanting to take over my life. And usually you don't irritate me. But right now . . . Jesus, Mari, do you think you could back off?"

She flinched back in her chair in shock. In six years, Duncan had never spoken to her like this. They'd always had a romantic, swoony kind of relationship, full of endearments and sappy little e-mails and kissy-faces over Skype. He'd swept her off her feet with expensive dinners at the Ivy and weekend getaways to Santa Barbara. He found her amusing and adorable, and never got impatient with her occasional dreamy fogginess—her creative mode—which drove most people crazy. But he understood, because he was an artist too, right?

"Duncan, I'm not trying to annoy you. I'm just concerned about my son. I want to make sure we're on the same page."

"I highly doubt that," he said brusquely. "Fortunately for him. But seriously, Mari, your timing sucks. I can't deal with this crap now. I've got a superstar rock group imploding on me, and you're bugging me about . . . what, again? I don't even know. Can we just finish dinner so I can get back and take care of this mess?"

Fury such as she had never known swept Maribel to her feet. "Consider it finished." She threw her car keys on the table. "I'll grab a cab."

"Mari, chill out. For God's sake."

She ignored him and made for the exit, afraid she'd throw his Portuguese bouillabaisse in his face if she stuck around any longer. She could put up with a lot—she did put up with a lot, probably too much, but that was another story—but she absolutely would not put up with someone dismissing Pete in such a callous way. It wasn't in her; she couldn't do it. Even for Duncan, who she . . .

But *did* she love him?

Luckily, a cab was just dropping someone off in front of the restaurant. She snagged it and gave the driver Kirk's address. She spent the drive fuming over Duncan's attitude. How could she marry him? How could she marry a man who thought Pete was just like any other little boy, that they were all the same, not worth the trouble of getting to know individually? The need to be with her son, her precious, one of a kind son, beat through her veins like a bongo drum.

Kirk opened the door with a finger to his lips. Barefoot, he wore drawstring workout pants and nothing else. His chest was a muscular blur in the dimmed light of his living room. "He fell asleep during *Hannah Montana*," he mouthed.

"*Hannah Montana?!*"

"I knew he'd think it was boring and I figured he needed some sleep."

"How'd you know?"

"What?"

"How'd you know he wouldn't like it?" She edged past him to check on Pete, who was sprawled on Kirk's blue-plaid sofa, his mouth open, eyes shut tight. With one part of her mind, she took note of Kirk's bachelor décor. With another, she realized Pete must really trust Kirk to fall asleep so deeply on his couch. But most of her mind was taken up with one all-consuming question. "Is it because all nine-year-old boys are the same?"

"What?" Kirk looked nervous. He ran his hand over the back of his neck, a gesture she'd seen him make before. "Of course not."

"Prove it."

"Excuse me?"

"What, am I being too demanding? Prove it!"

"Huh?" Poor Kirk seemed truly bewildered, and she couldn't blame him. She was bewildered herself. None of this had anything to do with Kirk. But for some reason she found it a lot easier to yell at him than at Duncan.

"Tell me why my son, Pete Boone, wouldn't enjoy an episode of *Hannah Montana*."

"Well," said Kirk slowly, as though drawing out each word in the hopes she'd calm down. "As you know, I'm sure, Pete's not really into music or TV or singing, which is what *Hannah Montana* is about. He's more into fantasy and magic-type stuff. He wanted to work on his book but he'd left it behind. He told me the plot. At length. Pretty cool, what I can remember."

She felt tears well in her eyes. In all the times Pete had told her the plot of his book, she rarely remembered the details either. They seemed to change too. It was a work in progress, as was her occasionally temperamental, sometimes fierce, always wonderful son.

"I'm done with Duncan," she said, almost choking on the words. "He doesn't deserve to be in Pete's life. And he can't have me without Pete, can he?"

Kirk went very still. Now that her eyes had adjusted to the light, she couldn't help staring at his bare chest. It was spectacular, though it looked as though a shark had taken three bites out of his torso. The wounds had scarred over, but they didn't affect his magnificence anyway. It was as if Michelangelo had returned to chisel a flesh-and-blood work of art. Ripped muscles ran in a syncopated pattern from the waistband of his pants to his taut shoulders. In the center of his chest, a light covering of blond fur begged to be petted.

"Sorry," Kirk said, pulling on a T-shirt. "When he fell asleep, I decided to work out for a bit. I'm still trying to get my strength back."

"That's okay," she said in a strangled voice. "It's fine with me."

"So you were saying, about Duncan."

Who? she almost asked. Then the temporary daze created by his bare chest wore off, and the memory came flooding back. "He thinks all nine-year-olds are alike. And he thinks I'm a haven. Translation: I'm supposed to shut up and not bother him."

"Are you sure about that?" Kirk gestured for her to follow him into the kitchen so they wouldn't wake Pete up.

She waited until they'd reached the cozy kitchen and he was pouring her a glass of water from the faucet. "You weren't there, watching him with his Brie and his bouillabaisse and his stupid phone."

"It's just that . . . never mind."

"What? Are you taking his side? What is it with you men? Maybe *you're* all alike!" She put down the glass of water with a click, the liquid sloshing onto the table.

"The word 'haven' doesn't sound like an insult, that's all."

"Forget it." She turned away, intent on collecting Pete and getting the hell out. Of course he didn't understand. Why should he? Just because he was nice to Pete and cared about dogs didn't mean he knew anything about her. Or cared, for that matter. "I'd better go."

"The hell with that," she heard him mutter through her blur of frustrated tears. Then strong arms came around her. Her feet were lifted off the ground. She was being held tight against a hot male chest.

Chapter Six

It was the wrong move. Of course it was. He was supposed to be showing her how much he respected her, not mauling her the second she dumped her fiancé. But she felt so good in his arms, a bundle of warm, sexy, tender woman. And the fact that she hadn't even blinked at the sight of his scars made him want her even more.

"Kirk!" She gaped at him, but she didn't look like she minded.

He stared down at her hazel eyes, noticing the way the gold-flecked irises had nearly disappeared as her pupils went wide and dark. "You're so beautiful," he said in a whisper.

Oddly, that statement seemed to confuse her. "You think I'm beautiful?"

"Why do you think I can never put two words together when I'm around you?"

Her mouth fell open, and that was that. He couldn't

resist a second longer. Lowering his head, he brushed his lips against hers, savoring the incredible softness of her mouth. It wasn't a kiss so much as a question, tender and tentative. Her lips tasted so sweet—was that coconut? What had she been eating at dinner with Duncan? The reminder of Duncan made him draw back. This was stupid. Asking for trouble. What if they'd just had an ordinary fight and would be back to normal by tomorrow?

Then she wrapped her arms around his neck and all regrets were obliterated. She grabbed him with passionate enthusiasm and suddenly her mouth was on his, hot and eager. This one wasn't a kiss so much as a statement. *I want you. I will have you.* He kissed her deeply, completely, irrevocably. Unable to get enough of her, he explored her mouth with his tongue: the slippery hardness of teeth, the pointed tip of her tongue, the delicious slickness of the roof of her mouth. She slipped out of his arms and pressed her entire body against him. He gripped her head in both his hands, tilting it to dive deep, to take her into him like air into lungs.

Then the rest of her body called to him, and he slid his hands down her sides, brushing the slight swell of her breasts crushed against him. He felt her shudder and nearly came in his workout pants. Speaking of which, she must be feeling every bit of his fierce erection pressed against her pelvis. All of a sudden he felt too exposed. All this time he'd hidden his longing for her. But you couldn't hide a boner the size of a tire iron behind a thin layer of cotton.

Not that she seemed to mind. She pushed her hips closer to him—*oh God!*—and made a moaning sound.

He got even harder and fought not to embarrass himself by coming all over her like a teenager under the bleachers. "Maribel," he forced himself to say, "I don't know about this."

"Why not?" Her breath was coming in quick, jagged gasps, and her glorious hair tumbled around her head like a halo of sunset. She looked like a fallen angel. "If you're worried about Pete, forget it. It practically takes a fire alarm to wake him up. You want me. I can tell."

He snorted, then groaned as the motion pushed his cock against the soft gap between her legs. "You think?"

Her eyes closed halfway, as if desire was dragging her eyelids down. "I want you too," she said, like a siren crooning to her next victim. "You can probably tell."

She put his hand on her breast and he wanted to weep, she felt so tempting. He caressed her soft, round apple of a breast, her aroused nipple nudging through her clothes. She was wearing a silky-looking dress with one of those peasant-type necklines, like a country wench in a tavern. It was held up by a ribbon tied in a bow right at the front, and lord help him, there was no possible way he could resist a gift-wrapped Maribel. His hand shaking slightly, he pulled the end of the bow and drew down her top so her breasts peeked out from a satiny, creamy nest of a bra. Her skin was one shade darker, more pink, than the bra, and a thousand times silkier. He drew his finger reverently across the rise of her breasts and into the dip between.

She gasped and leaned her upper half toward him. Color came and went in her cheeks. The knowledge that he was turning her on went to his head like a shot of vodka. He moved his hand to cup her breast, pulling down the edge of her bra with his thumb. Her nipple seemed to leap into his hand as if it belonged there, as if that velvety morsel was created to be touched by him. It swelled deliciously hard, begging for more attention.

He bent down, put his hands on her curvy ass, and picked her up, depositing her on the kitchen table.

"Oh!" she said, her mouth open in a shocked oval of surprise.

"You have no idea what you do to me," he muttered as he bent to her breasts, which were somehow, miraculously, both exposed now. Had he done that? Maybe he possessed magical powers of undressing women he wanted, women he . . . well, *loved*. No getting around it.

He gorged himself on her breasts as if they were snow cones on a hot day. Helped himself to her nipples as if they were chocolate-covered cherries. She threw her head back and let his hands roam at will, welcomed his ravaging tongue, writhed under the long sucklings of his mouth.

"That . . . feels . . . so incredible . . ." she panted. "Is there somewhere . . . else . . . ?"

He knew what she was trying to ask. They could go only so far on the kitchen table. Pete might be a sound sleeper, but then again, what if a fire alarm did go off? Catching his mother and his friendly neighborhood fireman screwing on the kitchen table might cause all kinds of nightmares.

His bedroom was just down the hall. It had a door. They could put something under the knob so no one could open it, so that if Pete woke up and wandered around looking for them, they'd have enough time to get decent before explaining that Kirk had been showing off his collection of . . .

A cold wave of sanity hit him. He couldn't let her inside his bedroom. Kirk closed his eyes, battling the drumbeat of lust and the throbbing of his cock. He'd started this, in a moment of sheer, panicked refusal to see her walk out of his kitchen. But if they didn't stop now, they'd end up in bed, and as much as he wanted that, she'd probably regret it quicker than a cat in a bathtub. He called upon all his higher angels, every speck of moral fiber, every ounce of the endurance he'd honed during chemotherapy.

And he firmly put her aside.

"Maribel." He gritted his teeth. "We can't do this. What about . . ." He cast around for something to throw cold water on the moment. "Duncan?"

"Duncan's a dick." She looked shocked at her words and clapped a hand over her mouth. "I didn't mean to say that." But his mention of her fiancé had done its intended job.

"Dick or not, he's probably waiting for you. Maybe he wants to apologize."

"He's probably sulking because I ditched him." She wrenched herself off the table and stalked around the kitchen, wringing her hands. "He sulks. He doesn't appreciate my son. He assumes I'm going to move to New York and stay home and be his haven."

Kirk prayed for the right words. The name Duncan, fortunately, had worked like magic on his erection. Time to start thinking with his head. The real one. "You don't want to move to New York?"

"No, I do. I think. I mean, I did. Oh fudge! What am I doing?" She squeezed her hands together in apparent agony.

"It's my fault. Don't blame yourself."

She cast him a skeptical glance. "Don't you dare let me off the hook here. I would have had sex with you on the kitchen floor."

Arousal pulsed again through his cock. *Focus, man, focus. Even if it hurts like a motherfucker.* He braced himself. "Do you love Duncan?"

Her face went flaming red. "I'm the wrong person to ask."

He let out a surprised snort of laughter. "Who else would know?"

"What I mean is, I'm not a big fan of love. I thought I loved Pete's father because his hair flopped over his forehead when he played the drums. It's important to know your flaws and shortcomings, right? I make bad decisions about men. I realize that. So I have to make decisions based on what's best for Pete."

He supposed that made sense, in an odd sort of way. And a tiny tendril of hope awoke in his heart. *She hadn't said that she loved Duncan.* "Okay, I can buy that. You're a single mother; you have to watch out for your son. So what is best for Pete?"

"Well, moving to New York, of course." She frowned,

giving him the impression she was trying to convince herself. "It's the greatest city in the world, after all. All the writers live there, and he loves to write. Publishers too. He'd get a much better education, especially because Duncan wants to send him to private school. Probably so he can make connections with famous people's kids, but even so. It's a great opportunity for Pete . . ." She trailed off.

"And what about you?" He made himself ask the question. "Are you excited about the move?"

"Sure!"

Maybe it was his imagination, but her cheerfulness seemed forced. And were her knuckles turning white as she gripped the edge of the kitchen counter behind her back? He felt bad, pushing her like this, interrogating her, but something told him she hadn't asked herself the tough questions. He waited patiently for her to continue.

"I'm ready for new horizons. San Gabriel's been wonderful, but I can't work at the Lazy Daisy forever, and it's not as if my photography career is taking off. I think I've sufficiently documented the jacarandas around here. Maybe it's time for subway tunnels and neon billboards." She looked forlornly around his kitchen, like a kitten caught in a storm. Suddenly she went still. Kirk followed her gaze. *Oops.*

MARIBEL STARED AT the abstract study of a yucca plant in bloom. The spiky red flowers looked like ominous red-painted claws. The long rays of the late-afternoon sun made every bulbous thorn stand out in horror-movie relief. It wasn't the most warm and fuzzy photo she'd ever taken. She'd been in a funk at the time. But here it was, framed and hung in Kirk's kitchen, right over a wall-mounted magnetic strip that held his kitchen knives.

Her eyes drifted to the hallway outside the kitchen. She could just make out the edge of a frame. Tilting her body to the left, she took in the sight of one of her pretentious black-and-white portraits of Mrs. Gund in her hairnet. Her boss stared sternly at the camera from the Lazy Daisy grill. Mrs. G. had actually paid her to take the photographs. They both knew it to be a mercy commission: Maribel had been facing some daunting medical bills after Pete had fallen off the roof during an unauthorized attempt to see if he could play Quidditch with the kitchen broom. Mrs. Gund had loved the photos and proudly displayed them in the coffee shop, but Maribel thought they were embarrassingly clichéd. Then, one by one, they'd been purchased.

Now here was one of them . . . no, two, she realized as she paced toward the hallway door. Three. Four. Five. All five. Except for the one Mrs. Gund had kept for herself. Five portraits of Mrs. Gund's impassive Norwegian face framed against various coffee-shop backdrops. The menu board. The coffee maker. The long counter. And so forth. The entire series—perhaps the low point of her creative learning curve—paraded down Kirk's hallway.

"You were the one who bought my Mrs. Gund photos," Maribel said numbly.

"Yes."

"Why? You can't possibly like them."

"Why not?"

"No one could. Except Mrs. Gund. Which I never understood, by the way."

She dared a look at Kirk. He was rubbing the back of his neck in what she now knew was a signal of discomfort. His intent, lustful look was gone, replaced by an awkward shifting of his eyes.

"I like them. Why else would I buy them? I like all your work."

Suddenly struck by a thought, Maribel dashed out of the kitchen.

"Wait," called Kirk, but she ignored him. She ran down the hall toward the open doorway at the end. Maybe it was rude to barge through someone's house like this. But she had to know.

Sure enough, there in his tidy blue-plaid bedroom, near the punching bag that swung from the ceiling, hung another of her photographs. At least she was proud of this one. A flash flood had crashed through the desert outside San Gabriel one rainy January, and she'd gotten an amazing shot of a drenched sparrow taking refuge on a cactus, clinging to the thorns with frantic little feet.

It wasn't the only work of art gracing Kirk's bedroom, but it was the most prominent. He also had a dreamy Irish landscape with two horses and a poster advertising the Rugby World Cup. Really, his décor was sad. From the bedside table came the low murmur of a police scanner.

"How come you never told me you were a fan of my

photography?" she asked without turning, knowing he was right behind her.

"I did."

"When, right between 'coffee' and 'black'?"

"I always buy your Christmas ornaments."

"That's different. Those are goofy little craft items I make for extra cash. This is my *art*." Duncan always laughed at her when she referred to her passion as art, but what the hell, Duncan wasn't here right now.

Kirk was looking slightly panicked. "Should we go check on Pete?"

"Forget about Pete. He's fine." Maybe she sounded like a heartless mother, but she knew her son. He'd probably sleep through a collision with an asteroid, then be really bummed that he'd missed it. "Wait! I know! You're just storing these here because Mrs. Gund ran out of room. It's not like you actually bought them all."

But Kirk raised reluctant, silver-smoked eyes to meet hers. "No. I bought them."

"But that's . . ." She tallied up the photographs she'd seen so far, added in the cost of framing, and flinched. "A lot of money."

"Over the years, maybe. It's not like I liquidated my savings or anything."

"Did you do it to help me out? Did I seem that desperate? The clichéd struggling single mom trying to make ends meet on a wing and a prayer?"

"That's not fair." He looked so hurt she instantly felt bad.

"You can't possibly like all those pieces. The sparrow,

I'll give you that one. It's one of my better efforts. But you can't convince me you always dreamed of having five portraits of an expressionless Norwegian coffee-shop owner filling your hallway."

His eyes darted around the room, as if looking desperately for escape. It occurred to her that she wouldn't get far in her career if she was this hard on everyone who bought one of her pieces. But . . . one, she could understand. Seven?

"Do you have others?"

"No. This is it."

She took a step back and folded her arms across her chest. "Do you think these will be worth something someday? I hate to break it to you, but the chances of that are very, very minuscule."

"They're worth something now." He flushed in a rather endearing way. "To me, anyway."

"Why?"

"Because . . . because they're . . . you. You made them. That's worth something."

She shook her head with disbelief. "You felt sorry for me. You knew I needed money. They were mercy purchases."

"No! *Damn!*"

He turned away and slammed a fist against the punching bag that hung in the corner. It spun away in a blur of red leather. When it swung back toward him, he sent it whirling again with another roundhouse punch. After a minute of this, a minute during which she berated herself for upsetting her one and only collector, he deliberately stopped the bag and turned to face her.

"Okay, I knew it would help you out, but that's not the only reason. I like looking at your photographs. I like the way you see things. I'm a fan. That's all."

"That's all?" It felt like something was missing, but the hell if she knew what. She frowned, oddly disappointed, and shrugged. "Okay, I guess. I'm flattered. To the best of my knowledge, you're my only fan. So, thanks."

He gave her a frazzled glance, like a drowning man watching the last lifeboat disappear. She took a step toward the door, more than ready to end this awkward scene.

"Wait! That's *not* all." There went his hand to the back of his neck again. "For God's sake, Maribel, don't you get it? I love your art. I love everything about you. I love *you*."

Chapter Seven

"WHAT?"

Now that Kirk's silent-type shell had cracked, he kept talking, as if he couldn't stop himself.

"I've loved you forever, it feels like. Since I don't know when. Early on. Why do you think we always come to the Lazy Daisy? But I couldn't have you. You were with someone. At first I figured it was a crush and it would go away. But it hasn't. I still feel it, more than ever."

She shook her head, trying to clear it, unable to grasp what he was saying. "That's why you bought my photographs?"

"I like them. I wanted to support your career because . . . I think you're really good. That's just my opinion, and I know I'm not an expert."

He looked so wretched, she couldn't stand it. "It's okay. I'm glad. I mean . . . I'm glad they're here." She gave one last wild glance around the bedroom. She thought about Duncan waiting at home, and what she'd almost done here, with Kirk. Who said he loved her.

But she couldn't think about that now. Couldn't take it in. "I have to go. In the living room, she scooped Pete up, barely managed a stammered goodbye, and fled. Thankfully, her son slept through the short wait for the cab, insertion into the cab, and the drive home, which gave her lots of time to lose herself in her windmilling thoughts.

For the last six years, she hadn't spent time with any man other than Duncan. Being with Kirk wasn't anything like being with Duncan. Kirk made her feel more—how to pin it down?—*interesting*. Duncan claimed to find her adorable and enchanting, not to mention his haven, but he tended to glaze over when she talked. This had never bothered her. He was a celebrity photographer, after all, and she was a teenage mom turned waitress turned amateur shutterbug. But now that they were really, as opposed to hypothetically, getting married, big alarm bells were going off right and left.

Duncan didn't inspire any sort of urge to have sex on a kitchen table. Duncan hadn't ever spent one dime on any of her photographs. Duncan didn't look at her as if he never wanted to stop. He didn't listen to her much at all. He'd certainly been in no hurry to get married; in fact, she still didn't know why he'd suddenly decided the time had come. Surely a free weekend in the Hamptons wasn't enough of a reason.

As the driver waited at a stoplight, she watched his digital clock change to midnight. She never stayed up this late, yet she was wide awake, as if she'd stuck her hand in a socket and every nerve had been jolted awake. And she knew it was because of Kirk. His kisses, his touch, his strength . . . his shocking declaration.

Don't think about that. It was too much to grasp. All this time, Kirk had been in love with her? How could she not have known? *Since I don't know when,* he'd said. A secret warmth filtered through her as she thought of all the times Kirk had come into the coffee shop. She'd always looked for him, been extra aware of him, felt a special zing when their hands brushed over a to-go cup and some change. She'd admitted to herself that she found him attractive, that she had a crush. But she'd never allowed herself to follow up on the idea. She was *engaged*. To a man who could have anyone but who wanted her. Her awe at Duncan's presence in her life had blinded her to everything else.

When the cab reached her house, she paid the driver and roused Pete enough so he could make it inside on his own two feet. He made a good zombie; she could probably make him brush his teeth, change into pajamas, and maybe even do some homework without him remembering a thing the next day. But her car was in the driveway and her bedroom lights were on, so she told Pete to go crawl into bed.

Confrontation with Duncan was at hand.

She heaved a sigh as she guided Pete toward his room. Oddly, she didn't feel guilty about anything that had happened with Kirk. She probably ought to, and she gave it a good effort, but it went nowhere. Kirk was . . . he was . . . he was magic. He made her feel like Wonder

Woman and Greta Garbo combined. He made her feel alive and desired and appreciated. Was that selfish? Maybe it was.

Maybe it was time to get a little selfish.

Duncan was waiting in her bed, working on his laptop. His silk striped pajama top was open at the neck, showing off the sunburn he always got when he came to San Gabriel. His mouth had a sullen cast to it, but as soon as he looked at her over the rims of his glasses, he shifted. He must have seen something unfamiliar in her expression, because he set aside the laptop and patted her side of the bed.

"I'm sorry I upset you," he said. "Can we give our little convo another chance, now that I'm not so distracted?"

"Our little convo?" She stayed in the doorway, unwilling to get any closer to him.

"You wanted to know why I thought we should get married."

"Right." Truthfully, other concerns had taken over by now, but that one still loomed.

"The thing is, I feel different when I'm with you, Mari. I don't have to prove anything. It's comfortable. Homey."

"Homey?"

Duncan shoved his glasses back up his face, looking uncharacteristically awkward. "That sounded all wrong. What I mean to say is, I want to come home to you. I've been giving all my attention to my career and only a tiny bit to you. Look at the way I was at dinner. I barely heard what you were saying; you were like an irritating buzz in my ear. I'm not proud of that, Maribel. If we get married, it won't be like that anymore. Don't you want to save me from being a hopeless workaholic?"

His usually charming smile fell flat. "So that's why you need me? To keep buzzing in your ear until you stop working?"

"Maribel. Don't be harsh. That's not you. You're always so lovely and soft; that's what I love about you."

"Duncan." Her abruptness took both of them by surprise; she even jumped a bit. "What do you think of my work?"

He blinked behind his horn-rims, like a blond, bland owl. "Your work?"

"Not my waitressing skills. My photography. What do you think, really? Your honest opinion."

"Not bad, if you like that sort of thing," he answered promptly. "Pretty good, in fact. Not my cup of tea, but I'm not ashamed to be marrying the creator." He offered a conspiratorial smile.

Not ashamed . . . hadn't she read about this in a psychology book? If he came up with the word "ashamed," then he was ashamed, no matter what he said. Or had been. Maybe he'd convinced himself he wasn't.

"Define 'that sort of thing.'"

"Excuse me?"

"That sort of thing. The sort you don't like but maybe other people do. What sort of thing? Come on, Dunc, it's not difficult."

"What's gotten into you, baby? You're not usually like this. And where did you go when you stormed out of the restaurant like that? I've been waiting for hours."

"Diversion tactic."

"What?"

Never had she been so grateful for her obsession with parenting books. Not that she'd ever imagined she'd be using her knowledge on Duncan.

"I'm not falling for your diversionary tactics. What sort of thing is it that I create?"

"Sweetie, it's not such a big deal. I like photographing people. You like nature. I find nature clichéd. But did you ever think it might be a good thing we're not in the same field? We're not competing against each other." He laughed, as if the entire idea of the two of them competing was, well, laughable.

She turned away, mostly to avoid throwing something at his smug face. Instantly he was out of the bed and striding to her side. He put his hands on her shoulders just the way Kirk had, but the shivers Duncan inspired felt more like spiders skittering up and down her arms. Time was, he'd been like a meteor streaking through her life at unpredictable moments. Where was all that dazzled, starstruck awe he used to inspire?

"Come on, baby, let's table this for tonight. I love you. I want to marry you. Still do, even though you walked out on a fabulous raspberry terrine."

"You stayed for dessert?"

"Ran into an old Exeter friend of mine. We hung out for a while and caught up on old times. What was I supposed to do? Crawl home and hide under the blankets? Watch Lifetime and gorge myself on Haagen-Dazs?"

She pushed his hands away. The very sight of him,

sandy-haired and self-satisfied, his mouth quirked to produce his supposedly witty quip, made her gag. "I'm going to check on Pete."

"Honey, we can get through this. After six years together, we can get through anything. Right?"

But as she gazed at the sleeping lump of her son, she wondered if they'd ever really been "together." He was never around when she really needed someone, and she'd never asked him to be. He'd been more of a glamorous god occasionally descending into her life. Never a partner or a helpmate.

Was that a basis for a marriage?

But the next morning, after a restless night sleeping next to Duncan, who kept trying to throw his leg over her thigh, she knew she wasn't ready to take any drastic steps. She needed to think things through before she made any irrevocable decisions.

Around nine, while she was making banana pancake batter, her phone rang. Electric thrills ran through her at the sight of Kirk's number. Duncan, still in his silk pajamas, was immersed in a new series of text messages and barely noticed when she answered, breathlessly, "Hello?"

"Maribel, it's Kirk." His voice, deep and resonant, brought to mind a quiet wind rustling pines in the forest. Her heart felt as if it would burst out of her throat, it was pounding so hard.

"How are you?"

"Embarrassed. Apologetic."

"No need. Really." She shot Duncan a surreptitious

look, but he was muttering furiously at his iPhone. "I'm the one who should be."

"I . . . uh . . ." He cleared his throat. "I wanted to let Pete know that I've located Gonzalez, Hagrid's former owner. He's in Colorado. I sent him an e-mail letting him know we found Hagrid, though I remembered his name used to be Z-boy. Short for Zeus."

"Zeus? Like the god Zeus?"

Duncan looked up, raising an eyebrow in curiosity.

"Yep. No idea why. Not sure why I forgot either, because the guys at the firehouse call me Thor, and Gonzalez always got a kick out of that. At any rate, I'll let Pete know as soon as I hear anything. For all we know, Gonzalez lost track of the dog and wants him back."

"Oh, that would be wonderful! I mean, if he could be reunited with his real owner. Even Pete would be okay with that." Pete was in his room, staging his usual late appearance at breakfast when Duncan was visiting.

"It seemed like a good solution all around."

"Thank you so much. I really appreciate it. Pete's gotten so attached to him in such a short amount of time." She bit her lip. Hagrid wasn't the only one Pete had gotten attached to.

"Maribel . . . wait, don't hang up. I've been beating myself up all night over the things I said."

"This isn't . . ." Feeling her face heat, she glanced at Duncan, who, mercifully, seemed oblivious to her embarrassment. "Wait, you're saying you didn't mean those things?"

"Oh, I meant them. Every word. And then some. But

I didn't mean to dump all that on you. You have enough to worry about."

"Oh."

He was doing it again, trying to spare other people the trouble of . . . what? Worrying about him? Caring about him? But she couldn't say all that, not with Duncan sitting right there in his tan-and-white—sorry, fawn-and-mint—striped silk.

"So don't feel awkward next time I come into the coffee shop, okay?"

"I won't. But . . ." She trailed off, hating the fact that she couldn't speak freely. Words choked in her throat like debris piling up at a dam.

"And don't feel funny about the photos. I think they're a good investment."

She murmured, "If you like that sort of thing." Duncan looked up sharply.

"So we okay?"

"Of course." She hung up numbly. Even the phone felt funny in her hands, as if the sensation of it was muffled. Duncan's voice seemed to come from some other planet.

"Who was that?"

"Oh, just a friend."

With a sidelong glance, she noticed the suspicious furrow between his eyebrows.

"Of Pete's."

"A friend of Pete's?"

"Well, of both of us. There's this dog, and Pete's really worried about him, and this fireman is helping find the owner, and . . ." But Duncan had apparently heard enough to realize he wasn't really that interested. He waved a hand and went back to his texting.

"I'm going to let Pete know the pancakes will be ready soon."

"Mmmhh."

She knocked on Pete's door, then went inside. Pete was, as usual, sprawled facedown on the floor, chewing on the end of his pen, his notebook under his chin.

"Pete, I . . . uh . . . Kirk called about Hagrid."

Pete looked up eagerly. "Yeah?"

"He might have found his original owner." When Pete scowled, she added, "That's good, right?"

"No."

"Why not?"

"His owner *abandoned* him, that's why not! He doesn't deserve to have him back."

Maribel walked all the way in and sat on his bed. "We don't know that. Maybe he just lost him."

"Same thing. If I had a great dog like Hagrid, I wouldn't *lose* him. That's just stupid. I bet Hagrid ran away from him. He's probably a big jerk."

"Pete. Let's give him a chance, huh?"

"You always say that. Give him a chance, give him a chance! I'm sick of giving people a chance. What difference does it make anyway? Nothing changes!"

Maribel knew what he was talking about. Duncan. How many times over the years had she urged Pete to give Duncan a chance?

"Sweetie, I know you don't really like Duncan. But he's been there for us, right? He's never walked away. That counts for something, doesn't it?" She didn't say out loud the other part of that thought—he'd never walked away, unlike Pete's father.

"No, it doesn't. He's never here to begin with. And when he is, he doesn't *do* anything. I mean, not anything fun."

"Like play wizards, for instance? Or Dungeons and Dragons?"

"Like *anything*," Pete said fiercely. "You can marry him if you want, but I don't have to talk to him. And I'm going to name the giant slug who lives in the Cave of Torment after him. You can't stop me."

"I guess not. Artistic license."

"And I'm naming the fire dragon Kirk."

"Because he's a fireman? That makes sense, I guess."

"No, not because he's a fireman. Don't you ever listen to my story? I have to tell the whole plot all over again! The fire dragon's really a nobleman, see? He was cursed by a witch who turned him into a dragon who gets burned by the sun. That's why he's a fire dragon—he catches on fire. It's really painful but he never cries. And no one understands what's happening to him, so they're scared of him, but he's really noble and kind and rescues people in the middle of the night when the sun can't burn him."

Maribel opened her mouth but couldn't speak a word. Kirk the Fire Dragon. Noble and kind. Burned from the sun.

Did Pete know about Kirk's cancer? Or had his imagination concocted a good reason for Kirk to work on his motorcycle in a place sheltered from the sun?

"Does he ... um ... what happens to Kirk the Dragon?"

"Mom, I don't know! I'm only on chapter three of Book One. And there's going to be at least seven books. But I know what happens to Duncan the Giant Slug. He's going to get squished. A big boulder is going to—"

"Okay, okay, I get it. Anyway, pancakes are just about ready, honey. And please don't squish Duncan until after breakfast, okay?"

"*Fine.*"

After she left Pete's room, unable to face Duncan yet, she took shelter in the bathroom. The scent of rose-petal potpourri greeted her, along with the sight of her pale face in the mirror.

The image of Kirk as a fire dragon pounded through her brain. It was eerily perfect. There was something else Pete had said, that it didn't matter that Duncan had never walked away, because he'd never really been around to begin with.

Abandonment wasn't the problem here. It had already happened. This time they'd been pre-abandoned by a distracted, self-absorbed workaholic.

But whose fault was that?

Maybe she'd never wanted Duncan around that much. Maybe that's why they'd lasted six years. They'd never had to confront anything difficult until now.

Maybe her son was right. Maybe she should have listened to him a little more. Maybe she needed to tear off her rose-colored glasses and get real.

Chapter Eight

KIRK HANDED THE keys of his Harley to Bruce, who'd answered his Craigslist ad.

"Take it easy. Speed limit's thirty-five around here. And I know all the cops."

"No worries, dude." Bruce, a young snowboarder from Tahoe, kick-started the Harley and grinned. "Suhweet. Be right back."

He roared off. Kirk leaned against his truck, which was already heating up from the morning sun. He ought to go inside, but the hell with it. Before long he'd be far away from the intense desert rays. Besides, he needed to conserve energy for the important stuff: packing and thinking about Maribel.

Two weeks had passed without a single encounter with her. Two crucial weeks during which Kirk felt something die inside him. He'd taken his shot. Bared his heart. Spilled his guts. He'd never done anything so tough in his life. Firefighter exam, chemotherapy, the decision to leave San Gabriel—it all paled next to the leap off a cliff he'd taken under Maribel's incredulous hazel gaze.

Bruce zoomed back into sight and veered into the driveway, stopping on a dime before he hit the truck. The kid could ride, no doubt about that. "You got all the maintenance records?"

"Yup. Not much there; it's been a good bike. Couple tune-ups, that's about it."

"Harleys, man. They don't need much." Bruce passed his hand reverently across the still-purring body. "Why you selling her again?"

"I have to leave town. Moving to Alaska."

"*Alaska?* You a snowboarder too?"

"No, no. I . . . uh . . ." Kirk eyed the guy's sunburned face. Wouldn't hurt to warn him. "I got skin cancer. It could come back. I decided I'd be better off somewhere where the angle of the sun isn't so direct. Alaska's so far north, the UV index is a lot lower." Bruce was goggling at him. "You wear sunscreen?"

"No."

"Tell you what. I'll give you two hundred dollars off the price of the Harley if you spend it all on sunscreen."

"Rad. Thanks, dude."

"So you want the bike?"

"Hellz yeah."

A couple thousand dollars richer, Kirk watched his bike ride off into the midday sun with Bruce the Snowboarder. It ought to make him sad, but it just added to the growing hole in his heart. One more snip of the ties binding him to San Gabriel and his old life.

His big regret was that he hadn't been able to give Pete one more ride on the bike before he sold it. He hadn't seen the kid since the night he babysat him. Every time he checked on Hagrid, he saw that someone had brought food for him. Maybe Maribel was bringing Pete to the warehouse. Or maybe Duncan was.

But he'd finally gotten an e-mail from Gonzalez and needed to share it with Pete, so he'd left a message for Maribel and any day . . . hour . . . minute . . . he'd hear back from one of them. And that would be the final loose end. One last beer with the guys, one last viewing of the desert sunset from the tailgate of his truck, and he'd be gone.

PETE WAITED TO call Kirk back until his mother had shut herself in her bedroom with her laptop. Ever since Duncan's last visit, things had been different. The wedding was off, along with the move to New York, even though she still talked to Duncan on the phone. And she'd been nice about driving out to see Hagrid—but mean about Kirk, saying she needed some time to sort everything out.

He had no idea what that meant, but if it meant less Duncan, he was all for it.

When he heard the sound of his mother's voice, Skyping from her bedroom, he dialed Kirk's number.

"Hi. It's Pete."

"Hey, buddy. I've got good news for you about Z-boy. Hagrid."

Pete's stomach dropped. Even though Kirk was cool, he was still a grown-up, and their ideas about good news always differed from his. "What is it?"

"Gonzalez e-mailed me. He didn't leave Z-boy behind on purpose. He said the dog jumped out of the truck when they left the shop. Ran away and wouldn't come back, no matter what they did. They stuck around for another day trying to lure him back with fried liver and bacon, all his favorites, but he didn't bite. They never saw him again. He was really happy to know we've been taking care of him."

Pete did a silent air-punch of glee. Hagrid had run away. That mean he wasn't Gonzalez's dog anymore. "Cool."

"There's more. He's willing to pay to ship Hagrid to Colorado if we can get him into a carrier. He's got a friend flying out of San Gabriel tomorrow; he can take him."

"What?"

"He misses Z-boy. Says he's a special dog. He told me his whole history. He was trained as a rescue dog for San Gabriel County Search and Rescue. Then he got injured in an earthquake rescue. Said he still has a limp, but I never noticed it."

Pete mumbled an answer. He'd noticed the limp right away, but that was because he cared about Hagrid so much.

"Anyway, they retired him with honors, and that's when Gonzalez adopted him. He has a plaque float-ing around somewhere. So I guess we have to convince Hagrid—Z-boy—to let us put him in a carrier. What do you say we go out and do it together?"

"No!" Pete burst out. "He doesn't want to go to Colorado. Why do you think he ran away?"

"Aw, Pete. Don't you think he probably misses Gonzalez?"

"No." If Hagrid had been so crazy about Gonzalez, he wouldn't have jumped out of the truck. Seemed obvious to Pete.

"Maybe you should talk to your mom about this. Maybe she has some good ideas."

"Nah." A lump of sheer resentment nearly choked him. "She's too busy all the time." He felt bad as soon as he said it. It's not that he was mad at his mother exactly. It wasn't her fault she was allergic to dogs. It wasn't her fault Duncan was such a douche bag.

"Wedding plans keeping her busy?" Kirk's voice sounded a little funny.

"No. They're not getting married. That's one good thing. He keeps calling though."

"Really? The wedding's off?"

"Don't tell her I told you. It's supposed to be a secret."

"Oh." A short silence followed. "So, about Hagrid. I told Gonzalez I'd try to deliver him to his friend tomorrow night. You want to go out to the warehouse tomorrow afternoon?"

"Um . . . I have to ask my mom."

"Sure. Let me know."

Pete hung up. Gonzalez didn't deserve to have Hagrid back. What would Harry Potter do in this situation? Or better yet, his own hero, Robin Dareheart, who had just discovered a magic stalagmite in the Cave of Torment that gave him the ability to change into any living being at any given moment? He'd never just sit back while disaster struck.

Tomorrow afternoon Kirk would be heading out to the warehouse. That gave him plenty of time.

LIFE AS THE former fiancée of Duncan Geller felt very odd, as if Maribel had just shed an outer layer of skin. On the one hand, she felt raw and vulnerable. Her relationship with Duncan had been a shockingly huge part of how she saw herself. She hadn't been just a waitress; she'd been the chosen one of the great celebrity photographer. It was as if her childhood blankie had been yanked away from her.

On the other hand, she knew she'd done the right thing. She felt lighter and more awake, as if her mind was filled with clear, sparkling water. She and Duncan were all wrong for each other. They had a certain amount of chemistry but nothing earthshaking. He patronized her, while she had spent countless hours listening to him, never admitting to herself how much he bored her. The only reason they hadn't figured it out earlier was that convenient three thousand miles between them.

"So stupid," she muttered as she refilled the cute little milk jugs of creamer that graced each table.

"What?" asked Mrs. Gund.

"Nothing."

She hadn't yet told Mrs. Gund she'd broken up with Duncan. That might unleash an onslaught of setup attempts with one or all of the Bachelor Firemen. Everything in her longed to run to Kirk, jump into his arms, tell him she was free and that the memory of his kisses hummed under her skin every moment of every day.

But she'd checked out a few books on breakups and knew the dangers of a rebound relationship. Better to give it some time, right? Let things settle down, let Duncan get all his over-analyzing out of his system, maybe do that therapy session by conference call he kept proposing. She felt awful hurting Duncan. She owed him a respectful breakup process, even if he did keep mentioning the shoot he had coming up with Lindsay Lohan as if that was supposed to make her jealous.

The door jingled open. Her heart jumped into her throat at the familiar sight of the dark blue T-shirts and suspenders of the Bachelor Firemen, even though she saw in an instant that neither one of them was Kirk. Ryan and the boyish-looking one they called Stud, but whose name was actually Fred, were walking toward the cash register. Her hands shaking, she put away the half-and-half and went out to take their order.

"Mornin', gorgeous," said Ryan with a wink.

"Back at you." She smiled widely at him. Ryan sure was a sight for sore eyes even for someone like her, who couldn't stop thinking about his quiet coworker.

"I'll have an espresso with lots of sugar. But you already knew that, didn't you?" He offered up his knee-weakening smile.

"Yup. And a cappuccino with cinnamon for you, Fred, right?"

Fred turned as red as the fire engine parked at the curb. "Right. Thanks."

She turned to the espresso machine. Not that she was counting the days or anything, but she hadn't seen Kirk in . . . well, since *that night*. She hoped he wasn't avoiding the Lazy Daisy so he didn't have to see her. He'd told her not to feel awkward, but what if he felt uncomfortable?

"Should I . . . um . . . throw in a black coffee for Kirk? I mean, Thor? Or is he off-shift today?"

"He's off-shift all right. His last day was Friday. Weird to see his locker emptied out." Ryan shook his head. "It's hard to see him go. He's like a brother. But at least he's . . ." He trailed off, as if he'd gone too far.

"Alive," said Fred helpfully. "Close thing too."

"Stud!" hissed Ryan.

Fred turned even redder. Maribel's thoughts were wheeling like a flock of surprised swallows. Kirk had left the firehouse? He'd never mentioned anything about leaving the station.

"Did he quit or something? Transfer somewhere else?"

Ryan and Fred exchanged glances. "He's leaving California," Ryan finally answered. "Going to Alaska. For the climate. It's a long story, but if you want to hear it, you'd better ask him."

Maribel dropped the espresso cup onto the floor, where it bounced on the non-skid rubber mat. Black liquid spilled onto her sneakers. "He never told me. Why didn't he tell me?" Was he really going to leave town and never say a word? "I'm going to strangle him."

"Hey." Ryan reached out a hand to her forearm. "Go easy on him, okay? He's been through a lot."

She shook him off and dashed from behind the counter, nearly tripping over the dropped espresso cup. "Be back later, Mrs. Gund."

"What?" Mrs. Gund squawked.

"Don't worry, we got you covered, Mrs. G.," said Ryan. "Cap wants us back in half an hour, but until then, we're all yours."

"Herregud!" Mrs. Gund clapped her hand over her mouth, though she was the only one in the room who had any idea what that meant.

Maribel flew out of the Lazy Daisy and into her car. She ripped off her apron and tossed it in the backseat—not making that mistake again. Too bad she couldn't commandeer the fire engine. If this was a romantic comedy movie, the guys would drive her to Kirk's, where she would tell him . . . something clever and touching, and they would hug and kiss and . . . dissolve to the next scene. Truth was, she didn't know what to say. All she knew was she had to see him. The thought of him leaving the state was unbearable. Plain freaking unbearable.

She banged on his door, ignoring the unacceptable sight of the moving van parked in the driveway.

It felt like forever until the door opened and the sight of Kirk filled her vision. He looked harassed and tired, his hair mussed, his eyes shadowed. He wore a threadbare, long-sleeved, faded blue shirt with a smudge of dust across the sleeve. His feet were bare. He was the sexiest thing she'd ever laid eyes on.

"How could you?" Her hurt spilled into the question, making an accusation out of it. She flung her arms in the air, but he caught her wrist before she could accidentally make contact. "Let go."

But he didn't. He held onto her arm, his eyes burning. "How could I what?"

"Leave! Without telling me!"

But he didn't look apologetic. If anything, he looked even angrier. "And you're the honest one here? How could you break up with Duncan without telling me?"

"What?" Her mouth fell open. "How did you know...? That's different!"

Kirk pulled her inside and shut the door. He crossed his arms over his chest. "Different how?"

"It's . . . it's personal." She wasn't ready to explain about Duncan and her all-over-the-place feelings.

It was as if a wall of ice came down over his face. "So I'm not entitled to know things about your personal life. Fine. We're even. Thanks for stopping by." He put his hand on her shoulder and spun her around toward the door. She ducked under his arm and spun herself right back.

"That's not what I meant."

One of his eyebrows rose in a question. "Let me have it then. What did you mean?"

"I meant . . ." Oh God. Why was it so hard to say the important things? But for six years she'd avoided saying the important things to Duncan, and look where that had gotten her. "I meant . . ." He was leaving. A moving van stood in his driveway. Hurt lurked in his silvery eyes.

She loved him.

"I meant," she continued in barely a whisper, "that I want to be with you. You're like this pool of beautiful sunshine in my heart, and every time I think of you I get happy, and believe me, that's a lot, I think about you all the time, but I didn't want you to be a rebound guy, not that you would be, but I wanted to make sure. So I was sort of . . . waiting . . . but then Ryan said you were moving to Alaska . . . *Alaska*, do you know how far away that is?"

"Maribel," said Kirk, his voice rough, his eyes gone deepest gray. "I took a job in a small town up there that needs someone to train their volunteers. If figure I'll be inside more and it'll be easier to avoid the sun that far north. The UV level is lower. It's still a risk. I'll always have to be careful. The doctors say the cancer could come back."

Tears clogged the back of her throat, tears at the thought of no more Kirk, at the thought that he'd nearly died, that he could still die. "I understand all that. But you would just leave without saying goodbye?"

"No." He reached in his back pocket and pulled out a sheaf of paper covered with tiny writing. "Here's my goodbye."

"A *letter*?"

"You know me. I'm not so good when it comes to talking. But it explains everything."

His wobbly smile was too much for her, the icing on the cake of his irresistibility. She threw herself into his arms. Well, technically, against his chest, but he quickly wrapped his strong arms around her. His heart beat fast against her chest, a rapid patter that told her he was just as rattled as she was. Being back in Kirk's arms felt wonderful, better than wonderful, like a miracle.

"I don't want your letter, Kirk," she murmured into his warm neck.

"You don't?"

"I want you. Right now. And later on too."

"You sure?" He leaned his head back to peer into her face. "What about the rebound thing?"

"Forget that. You're not a rebound guy. You're the guy I've had a crush on for years but never let myself admit it. The guy I want to make love to for the next twenty-four hours straight. The guy who's kind to children and animals and women and total strangers whose houses happened to catch fire. The guy who makes my heart want to dance right out of my body every time you touch me. The guy who . . ."

He silenced her with a deep, spine-tingling kiss. "All right. Not that I don't love listening to you, but is there any action to go with that talk?"

"See?" She rained kisses on his dear, tired, handsome face. "You love listening to me. I love that. That's important, right? I've had enough of not speaking up for myself. No more of that, no way. If you want to be with me, you have to care what I think. And want."

"Oh I care, all right." He lifted her legs, one by one, so they wrapped around his waist. "Especially if you happen to be wanting me."

"I am." Her voice came in a rough whisper. "Oh Kirk,

I am. So much. I'm sorry I didn't come right away, as soon as I knew that I . . ."

"That you what?" He sounded distracted, maybe because he was trying to kiss her neck as he made his way past packing cartons down the hall to his bedroom.

"Well, as soon as I thought I might love you."

"Might?" He kicked open the door to his bedroom, which, thank the lord, still held a bed. "Let's see if we can't do better than that."

Chapter Nine

NOW THAT KIRK had Maribel where he wanted her, where he'd dreamed of having her for so long, no way was he going to drop the ball. He whisked her into the bedroom as if she weighed less than a pillow and flung her onto his bed. Her glorious auburn hair tumbled around her ears as she looked up at him, eyes wide with delight, mouth gaping adorably.

He stood over her, feeling like Tarzan and a Viking marauder rolled into one. He was practically beating his chest. "Mind if I rip your clothes off now?" he said with rough-edged courtesy, so as to distinguish himself from his pillaging Scandinavian ancestors.

"Feel free," she laughed.

So he did. Off went the pale green T-shirt with the retro Cadillac printed on it. The bra underneath, which was some blurred shade of white that he'd never be able to identify again, seemed to melt under the intensity of his lust. Her lovely breasts—there they were, just as he'd remembered during his restless nighttime fantasies—the size of perfect new apples, just as juicy and perky as a man could want. His mouth watered at the sight of her hard little nipples, already erect before he'd even touched them. Her skin was so delectable, so smooth and faintly freckled here and there. After he lifted her legs to pull off her jeans and underwear—a vague shade of pink—he parted her legs in awe to find a fluffy patch of ginger curls simply begging for his tongue.

He obliged, of course, but not until he'd done a thorough taste test of the rest of her body. She was full of sensual puzzles. How could the skin over her bottom rib taste like vanilla, whereas the curve to her waist tasted like green apples? Why did she quiver when he swirled his tongue around her belly button, but flat-out moan when he explored the dip between her hipbones? He could swear that one nipple was slightly plumper than the other, but he had to keep switching from one to the other to make sure. That brought on a whole cascade of sounds from Maribel, every one of which acted like a shot of adrenaline to his rearing cock.

He was so hard he could hang a fireman's coat on his boner. And as he knelt over her, licking and savoring, it kept bumping against her satin skin, each little brush a fresh torment of temptation. He wanted to bury himself inside her, make her his in the primal, ancient way of men, feel her heat from the inside, hear her cries as she surrendered her body and heart to him.

But first he wanted her to know how much he felt for

her. His mouth had never been his best tool, word-wise, but now he put it to use loving every last inch of her. With hands, body, tongue, lips, he told her how much he loved her, how much she inspired him, how he'd lay down his life for her, how everything he had was hers. And when he finally allowed his tongue to brush against the delicate tissues hiding behind that soft puff of hair, her desperate writhing—and the death grip she had on his head—-told him he didn't have to wait another second.

He reared up and placed his cock at her entrance. So close, so close . . . then a moment of sanity surfaced and he flung himself off her as if he'd been electrocuted.

"What? What?" She sat up, wild-eyed. "What happened? Why'd you stop?"

"Condom," he gasped. "Protect. You. Safe." Yes, words had definitely deserted him; he was apparently doing his own version of "Me Tarzan, you Jane."

"Well, *hurry*!"

He hurried. He scrambled to his bedside table, where he usually kept a few condoms, then realized he'd packed everything up. Wallet. Where'd he put his wallet?

Maribel moaned. He dropped to his knees, cock bobbing in front of him, and scrabbled through his pockets to find his wallet. There, between his Visa card and his video-store punch card, sat one lone condom.

Maribel was kneeling on the bed, watching him anxiously, when he arose, now fully sheathed. She looked so beautiful, her sunset hair a crazy tangle, her hazel eyes foggy with desire, that he wished he had an ounce of artistic talent so he could attempt to capture a tiny portion of her glory.

"I love you, Maribel," he said with sudden soberness. "I'm not doing this casually, just so you know. This means everything to me."

"I know," she whispered. "I understand." She reached for him and drew him against her soft body as if welcoming him home after a long, dangerous journey.

They moved against each other with none of the usual first-time awkwardness. When she slid her legs apart, still kneeling on the bed, he put both hands on her ass and pulled her hard against his hips. With a gasp from her and a groan from him, they joined in a burst of star-spangled joy. When he thrust into her body, the warmth rushed through him like hot brandy on a cold winter's night.

Long, luscious moments passed as he immersed himself in the wonder of Maribel. He felt suspended in a world with no time, where all that existed was the feel of her body, the quick beat of her heart against his chest, her hot, panting breath in his ear, the scent of aroused woman, then the frantic, triumphant cries as she tilted over the edge into release. The butterfly tremors of her inner channel around his cock pulled him along with her and he surrendered, helplessly, to the shocking joy of exploding inside her body.

He muttered her name as he came, he who never said much during sex. Now he couldn't stop babbling things like, "So good . . . Maribel . . . sweetheart . . . oh God . . ." and probably other goofy nonsense stuff. She didn't seem to mind, holding him tight and laughing breathlessly as he poured himself, heart and soul, into her sweet body.

MARIBEL DRIFTED HAPPILY on a magic carpet through a sunshine landscape of golden sunflowers and capering clouds. It seemed absurd that such bliss could exist without her having known about it. She'd had sex before—obviously. But she hadn't had *this* before. This . . . insanely beautiful, heart-to-heart, soul-to-soul experience. It felt as if she and Kirk had somehow exchanged parts of themselves as they'd made love. Essential parts, parts that meant they now belonged to each other in some basic kind of way.

She sighed happily. She was a fool for love, that's what she was. Six years of trying to be smart, to be careful and make good choices, gone in a burst of gloriously orgasmic impulsiveness. But to hell with it. This was right. She knew it with every singing cell of her satisfied body.

Next to her, Kirk lay equally stunned, or perhaps asleep. She blew on his ear. "Kirk."

"Shh." He lifted a hand abruptly. She drew back, confused. That wasn't a very romantic afterglow kind of response. Then she saw he was listening closely to the low murmur of his police scanner.

"Sounds like there's some sort of fire out on Highway 90."

"Highway 90?" She sat up. "Where that warehouse is?"

"Yeah. A lot of other buildings too. Hang on." He got up and walked to the scanner, which sat balanced on the windowsill in the absence of a bedside table. With absolutely no apparent concern for his naked, scarred state, he leaned over and turned up the volume. Maribel experienced a wave of sheer awe at his physical condition, at the body that had withstood an assault of cancer and chemicals. The hollows of his pelvic bones probably dipped deeper than they used to. He probably moved with less energy. She hated the fact that she hadn't been there for his bout with chemo. As soon as she could, she was going to learn every detail of what he'd gone through.

The voice of the dispatcher intruded. The woman spoke fast, in a kind of code Maribel didn't understand. She caught the words "structure fire" and "three alarm," "incident report" and "uninhabited."

"Uninhabited. That's good, right?"

But Kirk didn't answer, waiting tensely until the address came through again. "Three thousand Highway 90." Then he wheeled on her. "It's the warehouse. Pete isn't out there, is he?"

"No, of course not. He's in school. Besides, he knows he's not supposed to go out there alone."

"You sure he's at school? I told him I was going to pick up Hagrid this afternoon and put him on a plane to Colorado."

Maribel got a sick feeling in her stomach. She scrambled to her feet and looked around for her purse. Kirk located it and tossed it at her. *Cell phone.* It was off. When had she turned it off? *Doesn't matter. Turn it on.* One unheard message. From Pete's school.

Kirk was already pulling on his clothes. Maribel's

hands were shaking so hard she could barely play the message. Kirk plucked the phone out of her hands and clicked on the speaker.

"Ms. Boone, this is Janet from San Gabriel Elementary. Your son Pete hasn't been seen here at school since this morning. Please give us a call as soon as you can and let us know if you took him home."

"Come on," said Kirk roughly. "Get dressed, we're going out there." He picked up his own phone and clicked a speed-dial key. "Captain Brody, it's Thor. That warehouse fire out on 90, there might be a kid inside. Nine-year-old boy going after a dog. Ten-four. I'm on my way."

He stuffed the cell phone in his pocket and helped Maribel finish dressing. "Do you want to stay here, honey? Captain Brody and the guys are on it, and they're the best. I want to be there because Pete knows me. But if it's too much for you—"

"I'm going," she said tensely.

"Okay." He didn't argue, as she was afraid he would. They ran through the house to the driveway, where her car was parked behind his older-model brown truck, blocking him in. "We can take your car, it'll be faster. Mind if I drive?"

She dug in her purse and threw him her keys. If she drove in this state of mind, every telephone pole between here and the warehouse would be in danger. She dashed for the passenger seat and fastened her seat belt.

Good thing too, because her little Volvo had never been driven like a race car in the Indy 500 before. In Kirk's hands, her car suddenly acquired powerful acceleration, precision turns, speed limit–obliterating velocity. They screamed down the highway. She wouldn't have been at all surprised to find a platoon of state troopers behind them by the time they'd reached the city limits. But luck was with them, and before long they spotted giant billows of black smoke belching above the horizon.

"Oh my God," she started chanting, a thick dread clutching at her throat. Her boy, all that black smoke . . . But he couldn't be there. It must be a mistake. She should call Janet back and make sure. She punched redial on her phone. When a woman answered, she babbled, "Pete Boone, I'm calling about Pete. Is he there?"

"Ms. Boone? We've been trying to reach you. We called your workplace number too. No, no one's seen Pete since lunch. Are you saying he's not with you?"

Maribel dropped the phone, all her focus now on the looming black cloud a half mile away . . . a quarter mile . . . down the next road . . . at the end of the—Oh good Lord!

A hellish sight waited at the end of the road. The warehouse was completely engulfed in a thick, toxic-looking mass of roiling smoke, lit by a red, eerie glow. Orange flames darted here and there, like flickering snakes' tongues. Several fire engines were parked at different angles around the building, and helmeted, tank-bearing firemen were dragging hoses and setting up ladders.

"This could be a hazmat situation," muttered Kirk, peering into the mess. "Who knows what chemicals are in there? See how they're staying upwind to be safe? You'd better stay here."

"But Pete—"

"I don't see his bike. He usually drops it right by the front door. See?" He pointed to the front door, which, amazingly, was still intact. The fire was concentrated toward the back of the building. The front step was empty; no little blue Schwinn. Maribel went faint from relief. Maybe Pete had gone to the Lazy Daisy, or home to work on his book. He'd get a consequence—scolding, no computer games, something big—but at least he wasn't caught in a toxic inferno.

"Do you have a scarf or something?" Kirk was asking.

"What? Why?"

"I don't have any gear with me."

"Gear? Kirk, you can't go in there." She clutched at him, absolutely appalled.

"I'm just going to check it out. I'm not going inside, don't worry. How about that apron?"

She reached into the backseat and tossed it to him. He folded it, wrapped it around the lower half of his face, then tied the strings at the back. Above the rough cotton, his gray-green eyes stared at her intently. He looked like a pirate or a spy. Then he waggled his eyebrows, completely ruining the effect and making her burst into hysterical giggles.

"Be right back," he said, muffled in cotton. "Keep the windows closed." And he was gone, dashing toward the horrible gushing smoke. She watched him until he disappeared behind a fire engine. Even through the glass windows, she heard the hollow roar of the fire, like a blowtorch multiplied to a monstrous size, and the occasional yells of the firemen. The stench drifted in—through the vents, maybe? She put her hand over her mouth, gagging a bit.

She found her cell phone and called the house. *Pick up, Pete. Come on, sweetie.* But the only answer was her own voice on the outgoing message. Next, the Lazy Daisy.

"Haf not seen him, Maribel. And I'm on my own, cannot talk."

"Sorry. Call me if he comes in, would you? I'm getting frantic."

"I vill."

She hung up and looked back at the fire, a fresh wave of panic sending flutters to her heart. Where was Pete? With a sudden chill of dread, she knew he'd come here. Maybe he'd left his bike somewhere else for once. Maybe it was even now being incinerated in a chemical bonfire . . .

She had to get to Pete. Get him out. She jumped out of the car. The sickening smell of the fire nearly knocked her off her feet. "Pete!" she yelled, running toward the warehouse. Her voice sounded weird, nearly inaudible over the vast roar of the fire. But she kept at it anyway, yelling "Pete, Pete," until someone slammed into her and swooped her off the ground.

"What the hell are you doing?" Kirk yelled in a hoarse voice. "I told you to stay in the car!" He held her against his chest while she struggled against him.

"Pete . . . not at home . . . can't find him," Maribel panted. "Have to find him."

"The guys are on it. They haven't seen a bike. No sign

of anyone. You're just going to get killed if you go in there."

"But Kirk . . ." Tears were flowing down her cheeks. "I know he's here. I just know it. Please. You have to listen to me."

He stilled, scrutinizing her face. Would he listen? Would someone, for once, hear her?

"Okay," he said, putting her back on her feet but keeping a tight grip on her arm. "But you can't run into a burning building. That's what firefighters are for. We'll circle around the edges. And you don't make a move without me. Here."

He pulled a red bandanna from his pocket and tied it around her mouth and nose. The soft cotton, with a pleasant tang of laundry detergent, was a balm after the nasty, harsh stench of the smoke. "I had this stashed in Engine 1. Now come on."

But before they'd taken more than a few steps, he squeezed her arm so tightly she yelped.

"Shh!"

He waited, stock-still, until Maribel heard it too. The sharp bark of a dog. "I think that's Hagrid. That's the bark a rescue dog makes when they've found something. Let's go."

He ran toward the sound, which didn't come from the building but from the birch woods behind it. She ran after him, keeping her hand over her mouth so the bandanna didn't slide off. Even though they gave the burning warehouse a wide berth, it was absolutely terrifying, like a grotesque smoke monster bellowing and thrashing.

In quick, fascinated glimpses, she saw yellow-suited fire-fighters brave the smoke, aiming streams of water into its depths. The flow of water looked puny compared to the crazed beast of fire, but the firemen seemed undaunted. They worked together seamlessly, at least to her eye. It occurred to her that Kirk would have been right there with them if he hadn't quit the department.

Awe at his courage—at their courage—battled with sheer relief that he wasn't risking his life at the moment.

At the edge of the woods, a small white blur raced toward them. Pete's little dog.

"Hagrid! Z-boy!" Kirk rushed toward him. Man and dog met halfway, the dog nipping eagerly at his leg. Maribel caught a glimpse of his dark brown eyes, bright with urgency. Then the little guy wheeled around and raced back into the woods.

Chapter Ten

SOMETHING WET WAS sliming Pete's cheek. He opened his eyes, then squinted them shut right away. A bright shaft of light from above had nearly blinded him. And what was that black slippery stuff all around him? He tried to struggle to his feet, but he kept sliding around in the mud.

The mud.

Memory flooded back. He'd been running through the woods, away from the sneaky-looking men who'd shown up at the warehouse, when the ground had disappeared from under him and everything had gone black. He must have fallen into some kind of hole, like a trap.

His heart raced. Where was he? Where were those men?

He lifted his head and listened. Should he try to climb out of the hole? Was it safe? What would Robin Dareheart do if he saw a bunch of creepy men with red plastic containers that smelled like gasoline?

Robin Dareheart probably wouldn't have run. At least he'd grabbed Hagrid, although he'd had to leave his bike behind. Maybe it was a good thing Hagrid hadn't wanted to get in the saddlebag he'd brought.

"Hagrid," he whispered. "Are you here?"

Then he remembered. Halfway between the warehouse and the woods, he'd heard a shout, then a sharp *pop*.

Hagrid had wormed out of his arms and raced back toward the warehouse, barking like a maniac. Terrified, Pete had kept running until he reached the woods, then kept on, going in wild zigzags, until blackness had swallowed him up.

He gave a sob. *Hagrid*. Hagrid must have gone back to attack those men, scare them away. He'd probably gotten shot. That *pop* must have been a gunshot, right? He was probably lying dead outside the warehouse while those horrible men set it on fire. The building was probably burned to a crisp by now and Hagrid, poor brave Hagrid . . .

A sharp bark made him jerk. That sounded like . . . Was Hagrid still alive?

"Hagrid, shh!" He spoke in a loud whisper that hopefully wouldn't carry too far in case the men were still out there.

Quick little scrabbling sounds came from overhead, followed by the thump of running footsteps. Oh no, the men were after Hagrid. He had to get out of here, had to help . . . He made his hands into claws and dug them into the muddy sides of the hole. The light wasn't too far above him, just a few feet. If he could grab onto a tree root or something . . . He craned his neck at the opening overhead. Something was blocking the light. He squinted.

A furry white head peered down at him and gave a soft bark. The footsteps were still coming after him.

"Hagrid! What are you doing, boy? Run and hide. Hide!"

Then another figure appeared next to the dog. "Pete, is that you?"

Kirk. Dizzy with relief, Pete slid back down to the bottom of the hole. "I'm down here. Are those men still here?"

"The firemen? Yep, they're here, but they're a little busy."

"No," said Pete, but it didn't seem worth explaining right now. "I'm kind of stuck down here."

"So I see. Hang tight, I'll get a rope. You okay for a few more minutes?"

"Oh sure. Take your time." Now that Kirk and Hagrid were here, all fear left him. Kirk disappeared, but then his mother knelt next to Hagrid, the sunlight making a red halo out of her hair.

"Pete! Are you hurt?" She'd obviously been crying; he could tell from her voice. And he felt horrible all of a sudden. He'd snuck out of school, broken the rules, been shot at, nearly gotten Hagrid killed.

"No," he said in a thin voice. He hadn't felt like crying until this very moment. But now . . . "I'm not hurt. And I'm really sorry, Mom. You can ground me. I don't mind."

"Oh sweetie. You look pretty grounded already." She went for a laugh, which partly worked.

She'd made a joke. His mom, who must have been freaking out, had tried to make him laugh. Tears sprang out of his eyes. He wiped them away, getting mud all over his face.

His mother sneezed.

"Mom, you'd better get away from Hagrid. He's making you sneeze."

"Not yet. We're fine for now, me and Hagrid." He saw a movement up above that looked like a pat on the dog's head.

"You're going to have to take a bath when we get home," he said.

"I have a feeling I'm not the only one. Just how muddy are you?"

"About as muddy as the giant slug in the Cave of Torment."

"Wow! But sorry, I don't think we have a bathtub big enough for the giant slug."

Another joke! Everything was going to be okay. And then Kirk was back, and he knew for sure that everything would be fine.

"Okay, buddy. Time to show off your climbing skills." A rope, knotted at the end so he could easily grip it, slowly made its way down the hole. "You can tie it around your waist or just hold on."

"My hands are really muddy."

"Then tie it around your chest, under your arms. No hurry, Pete. Take your time, tie a good knot. That's right. Good job."

Kirk's calm voice made all the difference. Pete wasn't

nervous at all as he tied the knot.. He felt a little goofy dangling from the rope as Kirk hauled him up. He used his feet to hold himself off the sides of the hole. As his head cleared the opening, the first thing he felt was Hagrid's enthusiastic, joyful licking of every inch of his face. Next came his mother's arms, scooping him up tight, never mind the mud all over him. And then the unfamiliar, reassuring weight of a strong male hand clapping him on the back.

MARIBEL COULD BARELY stand to hear the details of Pete's adventure. A rescue ambulance came and paramedics checked him out and wrapped him in a blanket. Even though it was eighty degrees outside, her son kept shivering. Shock, they said. Luckily, they didn't feel a trip to Good Samaritan hospital was necessary. She stayed with Pete, sitting close to him on the tailgate of the rescue ambulance, and listened to the details of his story. He'd planned to stash Hagrid in the garden shed behind their house. Since she never did anything resembling yard work, it might have worked, if Hagrid had never barked or ventured outside during daylight hours.

"Honey, I wish we could keep Hagrid. I really do. But—"

"I know. It was stupid. I don't care anymore. I mean, I care, but I'm just glad he's alive."

They both glanced over at poor Hagrid, whose ear was being swathed in ointment by Fred, who'd spread out a blanket on the grass to tend to the dog. The fire was now a smoldering shadow of its former terrifying self, and the firefighters were putting away their equipment. A few of the fire engines had already left, but the San Gabriel crew was still there.

"He's a great dog," said Maribel softly. "You were right, Pete. He's special."

Pete nodded wearily. She wanted to throw up at the thought of everything he'd gone through—gunshots, arson-witnessing, getting knocked unconscious. She put her arm around him, wondering how she was ever going to let him out of her sight again.

Captain Brody walked over to them and surveyed Pete with sober charcoal-gray eyes. "Pete, the arson investigators are going to want to talk to you. Are you okay with that?"

"Why?" Maribel asked in alarm. "He's just a kid."

"But he's a smart kid. If he saw something that might help locate the arsonists, we might be able to lock them up so they don't do anything like this again. We might not even know it was arson if Pete hadn't seen as much as he did. These are dangerous people, professionals probably hired by the owners when they couldn't find a new renter It's not only arson, but attempted murder."

The blood drained from Maribel's face. She hadn't thought of it in those terms. "And Pete's the witness? But he didn't see anything. And they didn't see him, did they, Pete? Just from the back while you were running into the woods?"

Pete's eyes were wide with fright. "I don't think they saw my face."

"Don't worry, they'll never know his name. He'll be protected."

"Yes, he will be," said Kirk, stepping to Brody's side. His face looked grim and angry, his eyes like chips of quartz in a wall of granite. "I'll make sure of that."

Maribel was so glad to see him, she forgot that no one else knew they were—well, in love—and clutched his hand to her heart. "Kirk, where've you been?"

"Trying to figure out what happened. I'm guessing Hagrid went after the bastard—excuse me—who shot at Pete. Some gasoline spilled on his ear and a spark must have landed on it. That's one lucky dog."

"Brave too," said Captain Brody. He knelt on the blanket next to Fred and looked Hagrid in the eye. Hagrid gazed back with soulful brown eyes. .

"Good dog," said Brody finally, reaching out to scratch Hagrid's uninjured ear. "You did good. But you know that. I hear you were a helluva rescue dog."

Hagrid gave a soft yip and licked at Brody's hand.

"His ear isn't too bad," said Fred. "As long as it doesn't get infected, he should heal pretty quick. It's going to scar up though."

"Hear that, pup?" said Brody. "A battle scar. All the girls will love you."

Hagrid's intelligent gaze traveled from face to face, but always went back to Brody. He must have recognized the top dog in this pack of firefighters.

Brody scratched the dog under the chin, making his eyes close in bliss. "We'll have to make sure you're well taken care of, won't we?"

Pete piped up. "He doesn't want to go to Colorado. He's a California dog."

"Is that right?" The captain didn't seem to think it strange that Pete would speak for Hagrid. "Then again, maybe his work here is done." Another long moment of communion with Hagrid followed, while Maribel fought back tears. If Hagrid had been killed in the fire, or by the arsonists, would they have found Pete in that old sinkhole?

She held tightly to the lifeline of Kirk's hand. The warmth of his body, standing so close to her, felt more than reassuring; it felt essential.

Pete, apparently jealous of Hagrid's newfound dog-crush on Captain Brody, hopped down from the ambulance and knelt next to Hagrid. He kept the blanket wrapped around himself, but Maribel could tell he felt better. She snuggled closer to Kirk and rubbed her cheek on his arm.

"What did you mean when you said you'll make sure Pete's protected?" Maribel murmured.

"I'm going to make sure. Personally. I'm going to stay and watch over him."

"*What?*"

"Listen to me." She let him pull her away from the ambulance, out of Pete's earshot. "The police will probably offer some protection, depending on what the arson squad determines. But it's not enough. I'll sleep on your couch. I'll drive him to school. I'll check with the school officials about security there. I'll be his personal body-guard until the danger's passed."

"Kirk! That's crazy. You're supposed to be moving to Alaska."

A stubborn look came over his face, a very Thor-like expression that really ought to be accompanied by a thunderbolt. "Pete might be the only witness to arson and attempted murder. What's to stop them from trying to finish the job?"

Maribel shuddered. "But they didn't see him!"

"We don't know that. What if they had someone on lookout in the woods? We can't take a chance."

"But the police—"

"Are perfectly competent. But I'm not going to leave it up to them."

"Kirk . . ." She wrung her hands together. "You're scaring me. Of course. That's it: you're catastrophizing!"

"Maribel. Look at me." She did, and the dead-serious look in his eyes sent a chill straight through her. "I'm not catastrophizing. I'm being smart and careful. In fact, it would be even better if . . ."

"If what?"

But they were interrupted by Pete running toward them. "Hagrid might get a special award! Captain Brody says he's earned it."

"That's great, honey. Of course he's earned it."

Pete looked from one to the other of them. "What's wrong?"

"Sweetie, would you mind if Kirk stayed at our house for a little while?"

An exuberant hug around Kirk's waist, blanket sliding to the ground, was answer enough for Maribel.

"Fine," she told Kirk. "But we need to talk more about this."

That stubborn thunderbolt look came back, but he nodded. "What about Hagrid?" He turned to the captain. "Maribel's allergic. Any ideas who could take care of him for now?"

Brody stroked his stubbled chin thoughtfully. "I'll take him to the station, see if any of the crew wants to take him home. I'm sure we'll get some takers. Maybe even a bidding war. When everyone hears his story, they'll be fighting over who gets to adopt him."

"What about you, Cap? He really likes you." Hagrid had torn himself away from Fred's ministrations and was plastered to Brody's leg, gazing up at him adoringly.

"Not a good time," he said vaguely. "Rebecca, you know, well . . . not a good time." He strode toward Engine 1, Hagrid trotting eagerly at his feet. They watched the dog hop into the fire engine as if he'd been doing it for years. Maybe he had been, in his former career. Hagrid had many secrets, Maribel realized.

"Well." She took in a deep breath and smiled at her son and her . . . Kirk. "Shall we go home?"

KIRK PASSED AN uncomfortable night on Maribel's royal-purple overstuffed couch. After she'd put Pete to bed, she'd cuddled with him and things had gotten interesting, but neither had felt comfortable going any further with Pete liable to wake up any minute from a nightmare. Which he'd done, later on. Kirk heard Maribel slip into his room, heard the murmur of her voice soothing him, the soft lullaby she sang him. His heart hurt from the beauty of it. Everything he wanted was in that room. Maribel, a family, a bright boy, love, warmth, life. Nothing was going to hurt anyone in that room, he vowed; he'd give his own life to make sure.

The next day, Pete stayed home from school. Kirk had to go back to his house to move the last few boxes out. He called the movers and put everything on hold for a week. He'd have to talk to the police about their take on the situation. How would he know when it was safe to relax? Would he ever feel comfortable about Pete's safety, especially when he was thousands of miles away? He doubted that would ever happen. He'd have to consider canceling the move to Alaska.

When he got back to Maribel's house, she met him with a tender smile and a happy-to-see-you hug. "Pete's asleep in my room," she whispered. "Out like a light. We've got hours until he wakes up." She tugged him toward the living-room couch. He sank into its soft cushions with a sigh that seemed to come straight from his core. She knelt next to him, nudging him to twist a bit to the side. Then cool, gentle hands were playing across the back of his neck, stroking his tight muscles, rubbing out the knots of tension. His eyes drifted halfway shut at the pleasure of her caresses, the sweetness of being taken care of.

When he thought he'd reached a state of unmatchable bliss, it got better. Those sweet little hands reached around his front and tugged his shirt up. He raised his hands like a child, although the lower half of his body was all adult. The X-rated kind of adult. In no time flat.

She seemed happy about that sudden bulge in his jeans, if her next actions were any indication. Slipping off the couch, she came around in front of him and straddled his lap. Her cottony pink skirt flowed over his legs. It was like having a summer flower sit on him.

"Lie back, you stud. It's my turn." Her voice was huskier than usual, and he noticed an extra wash of pink on her round cheeks. Since resistance seemed pointless, he lay back and let her run her hands over his chest, her expression rapt as a kid at Christmas. Her light touch made his senses swim; it was as if she were a blind person reading him with her fingers. He closed his eyes. Instantly, his whole world shrank to the tracking of her every move, anticipation of her next exploration.

Her fingers discovered everything: the two chunks of missing flesh, the biopsy scar, the swirls of hair around his nipples, the skipping of the pulse in his neck, the way his very heartbeat danced to her touch. Her hands did more than discover; love flowed from her fingers through his ravaged skin into his heart, which seemed to expand into an unbearably bright sun, an inside sun that could never hurt him.

"You, my dear," she murmured as she trailed her hands to the top button of his jeans, "are one fine fireman."

"Is that right?" His voice was hoarse.

"Oh yes."

Her voice now came from the region of his crotch. He

jerked his eyes open to find her kneeling between his legs, unzipping his jeans. "What are you doing?"

"I'm sure you've heard of it." She smiled up at him, her pink lips already parted.

"Yes, but . . . you don't have to."

"Look, buster." She narrowed her eyes at him. "I love every piece of you, and I want to show you just how much. I don't want to hold back or tiptoe around you or hide what I want. If you have a problem with any of that, you'd better tell me right now."

"No. No. I . . . uh . . . no problem."

"Then zip it. Not this"—she reached inside his fly—"but that." She gave his mouth a scolding look, then wrapped her precious lips around his cock.

Oh sweet lord. *Give it up, Kirk. This woman owns you.* Scraps of thoughts flew through his brain as she moved her warm mouth up and down his shaft. Anything . . . forever . . . I'm yours . . . so good . . . Oh God . . . Maribel . . . inside . . . need . . . now . . .

When she paused for breath, he swooped in and whirled her onto the couch. "I've got to be inside you."

Maribel gave a little gasp, staring dizzily up at the man who'd been at her mercy one second ago. Now he braced himself over her, every ripped muscle vibrating with tension, his voice gritty from lust. She could just about faint from the desire written in every line of his usually serious face. It looked as though the restraint had been scorched out of him by raw, white-hot need.

"I want you, Maribel."

"Oh, me too." She brought his hand under her skirt,

between her legs. She knew he'd find her wet and ready. Loving him with her mouth, feeling his instant response, the swell and surge of him, was an incredible turn-on. He practically ripped her panties down her legs. That sudden show of strength made her gasp again. Then his hands were on her, those work-roughened, all-knowing hands. She nearly moaned from the happiness of having him touch her again. When was that first time . . . yesterday? It felt like eons had passed.

But it didn't matter; they were together again, hands on flesh, skin against damp skin, lips on mouth, heart against heart, him inside her, her around him.

She wrapped her legs around his hips, reveling in their power as he thrust into her body. Each flex of his hips set off a sparkling fountain of pleasure, each one deeper and sweeter and more piercing. "I love you, Kirk," she chanted in a whisper. "I love you, I love you."

She had no choice; her body, soul, and heart pushed the words out of her.

His answer seemed torn from the deepest part of himself. "Oh sweetheart. God, how I love you, Maribel."

And then great waves of pleasure lifted them up and away, spun them around, and launched them into endless, exquisite wonder.

Afterwards, they went into her sunny kitchen, where she put him in the chair farthest from the window and brought him coffee. "Coffee, black?" she asked, her voice still adorably sex-husky.

"Like old times." He smiled at her over the mug, blinking like a lovesick puppy.

She sat across from him, her pink skirt floating around her. He'd never forget that skirt.

"Pete and I are supposed to meet with the arson investigator tomorrow. Do you think you could come?"

The request made his heart glow. "Of course. Pete's not going anywhere without me for a while. I told you."

With a nervous, sidelong look, she plucked at the fabric of her skirt. "Kirk, while you were gone, Pete and I talked. We don't like what you're doing. It's not right."

Now that was a punch in the gut. He put the coffee mug down on the rickety side table by the couch. "Don't start, Maribel. You're not going to change my mind."

"But Kirk, have you forgotten you're *moving*? You're supposed to stay out of the sun, and it's nothing but sun here. It's bad for your health. We can't accept that."

Agitated, Kirk jumped to his feet. Maribel stood as well, arms folded, her hair a rumpled tangle around her head.

"It's my choice. I'm at risk either way, whether I move or don't. It won't kill me to stay a little longer."

"But you said the UV level is higher here."

"I'll take the chance, Maribel. I stay covered up, I use sunscreen. But I'm not taking chances with Pete's life. I won't. Don't ask me to, sweetheart." He took her by the shoulders, willing her to understand. "Last night I lay on your couch and promised myself I wouldn't let anything happen to you or Pete, if I can do anything to stop it. Nothing matters to me more than the two of you."

Tears swam in her wide hazel eyes, hung on her eyelashes. Fiercely, she dashed them away and glared up at him. "Don't you get it, Kirk? We don't want anything to happen to you either! We want to come with you to Alaska." Her face went pink as a peach. "I mean, if you want us."

"Wh . . . what?" He clutched her tighter, not sure he'd heard right. "Come to Alaska?"

"Ye . . . es." Her gaze dropped away, as if she was embarrassed. "I asked Pete how he'd feel about going with you. I said, 'I'm sorry you can't have a dog, but what about a fireman instead?' Kind of joking, you know. I explained that I loved you, and that you'd said you loved me too, and asked what he'd think of us all being together as a family and moving to Alaska and—are you okay?"

Sure, he was okay, as long as breathing wasn't absolutely essential. He managed to choke out some words. "What did he say?"

"He loves the idea," she said simply. "He thinks you're the best thing on two feet. Hagrid's the best on four, of course. Oof!"

He didn't remember how it happened, exactly, but he was suddenly squeezing the breath out of her, making her laugh and hug him back in a blaze of bright, shining joy that threatened to lift the little house off its foundations and float all the way to Alaska.

Fairness compelled him to double-check, though. "Are you sure? All the way to Alaska? I never thought . . ."

"It'll be an adventure," she said firmly. "I'll expand my artistic horizons and Pete can work some other climate zones into his epic novel. And we'll be safe from . . . you know. They're not going to hunt him down in Alaska. And, most important, we'll be with you."

True.

Of course, they'd have to discuss a wedding, or at least an engagement, but for now it was enough to hold her tight and feel happiness seep like a healing balm through every cell of his body.

KIRK BROUGHT PETE to the firehouse with him to say goodbye. Maribel was training her replacement at the Lazy Daisy but sent along a few dozen farewell muffins, everything but bran. All the Bachelor Firemen and the newest female member of the crew, the pretty, turquoise-eyed Sabina Jones, gathered around to shake his hand, clap his shoulder, and offer hugs. After the milling and chattering had died down, Captain Brody cleared his throat for attention. Hagrid was at his feet; his ear already looked nearly healed. Pete dropped down to pet him and scratch his neck until his tail threatened to pound a groove into the floor.

"The crew has voted. We all feel—unanimously—that the fairest thing to do with a dog as brave and fearless around fire as this one is to turn him into a firehouse dog. We checked with Gonzalez in Colorado and he's fine with it. So if it's okay with you, Pete, we'd like to adopt Hagrid here at San Gabriel Station 1."

"Really?" Pete looked up from his mutual adoration-fest with Hagrid.

"Yes. But I have to tell you, there's a catch."

"What?"

Kirk started to smile. He knew exactly what was coming.

"According to tradition, every firehouse dog here at Station 1 has been named Constancia. After Constancia B. Sidwell."

"Ill-fated bride of Virgil Rush, who left him in the lurch and inspired our bachelor curse," explained Ryan with a wink. "Which some of us call a blessing in disguise."

"Constancia? That's a horrible name!" Pete cried, appalled. "He's a boy, first of all."

"Good point. Besides, he just doesn't look like a Constancia to me. It's a bit old-fashioned. What do you say to the name Stan?"

"Stan," muttered Pete, stroking the dog's floppy ear. "Good boy, Stan, good boy." Hagrid/Z-boy/Stan cocked his head in answer. "That's fine. He's okay with Stan."

"Stan it is."

A cheer went up from the firefighters. Captain Brody smiled broadly. As Pete got to his feet, the captain clapped him on the shoulder. "You can visit him any time."

Ryan elbowed his way through the crowd. "You'll probably hear about him on the news way before that."

"Why?" Pete asked. "Because he's such a hero?"

"No, not that. We're going to spread it around that two dogs were at the scene and Stan slept through the fire. Throw off the arsonists. Nope, Stan's going to be known as the official Bachelor Fire Dog of San Gabriel. Now he'll never find a Mrs. Stan."

Sabina snorted and rolled her eyes. "You guys don't really believe in that curse, do you?"

Quiet descended.

"Anyone else notice how Kirk didn't hook up with Maribel until after he quit the department?" Vader said in a spooked voice.

"Hey," Kirk protested, with a quick glance at Pete. "We didn't 'hook up.' We're getting married."

The firemen let loose another round of cheers and hoots, before quieting again. "Weird, though," said Vader, as though telling a ghost story. "Six years without saying ten words at a time to her—"

"Record was seventeen," Fred pointed out. "Last Christmas. Sixteen on July 13."

Vader ignored him. "And suddenly, they're getting married. Makes you wonder."

"No, it doesn't," said Brody firmly. "Back to work, everyone. Pete, Kirk . . . good luck in Alaska. Keep in touch."

"Will do, Cap."

One last bear hug from the best captain he'd ever known, a last wave of goodbyes, one more lingering cuddle with Stan the Bachelor Fire Dog, and Kirk and Pete headed home, where Maribel, the moving van, and life itself awaited.

Want to see more of Stan the Dog
and the Bachelor Firemen of San Gabriel?

**Turn the page for excerpts from
the other Bachelor Firemen novels
by Jennifer Bernard
from Avon Books**

An Excerpt from

THE FIREMAN WHO LOVED ME

HOT MEN FOR A GREAT CAUSE.

The words on the poster were black, the background an orange fireball, and, front and center, a hunky fireman gripped his hose.

In the crowded lobby of the San Gabriel Hilton, Melissa McGuire stopped dead at the sight of the poster propped on the large easel. This couldn't possibly be right. She and her grandmother must have gotten their wires crossed. On Nelly's birthday, they usually gorged on hot butterscotch sundaes or the all-you-can-eat lunch buffet at the Bombay Deluxe. Had she misread "Hilton"? What else started with an H? Hooters? That seemed even more unlikely. But with Nelly, you never did know.

As she dug in her jeans pocket for the envelope on which Nelly had scrawled the directions, someone jostled her from behind.

"Hey!" she protested.

Oblivious, a pack of girls streamed past her, a blur of cropped tops and streaked hair. Now that she thought about it, the crowd was made up entirely of young women in their twenties and thirties. They were virtually stampeding in the direction of the ballroom. The last time Melissa had been here, she'd been covering the mayor's victory party for Channel Six. This had to be a mistake.

The envelope, when she finally found it, said otherwise. *San Gabriel Hilton, five p.m. I'll save us a seat at the front of the ballroom. Your loving grandmother, Nelly.* "Loving" was underlined twice. That meant trouble.

Melissa stumbled as a sharp elbow to her back nearly knocked her over. "Do you mind?"

"Oops, sorry," said a girl in a glitter-sprinkled party dress. "But all the good seats are going to be taken if we don't hurry."

Melissa took a step back. "What kind of event is this, anyway?" Whatever it was, it wasn't worth getting kneecapped over.

"Just get yourself a table up close and you won't be sorry." The girl disappeared into the crowd bottlenecked at the ballroom's double doors. A hum of chatter filled the lobby, rising and falling like swallows on an air current.

What had she stumbled into? Rather, what had her "loving" (translation, bossy and interfering) grandmother led her into? There was more text on that poster, if she could just get close enough to read it.

Two bruised ribs and a stubbed toe later, she stood in front of the easel. The silhouetted fireman in the poster looked so . . . manly. So heroic. A dynamo captured in mid-rescue. An ode to testosterone. It took her a moment to tear her eyes away and read the rest of the text. When she did, it took another moment for it to sink in.

The San Gabriel County Firefighter and Law Enforcement Officers Fourth Annual Bachelor Auction.

NELLY MCGUIRE SAT triumphantly at a linen-draped table right next to the ballroom stage. Her quilted purse was planted on the chair next to her. Inside it nestled tonight's program, which listed the bachelors who would be strutting their stuff that evening. She'd already underlined several names. The purse also contained a thick roll of hundred-dollar bills. It was a substantial chunk of her savings, but money well spent if it got Melissa a man before she, Nelly McGuire, kicked the bucket. Which would be sooner than—

"Excuse me, missy," she snapped as a shapely arm clad in white spandex reached for the chair with her purse on it. "That seat's taken."

"Excuuuuse me! Aren't you in the wrong place, Granny? Bingo's down the street." A smirk dented the girl's glossy, pouting mouth. Nelly had to admit she was gorgeous. All the more reason to cut her down to size.

"I'm here at the invitation of my grandson. He told me to sit right up front, so I could make sure no worthless hussy bids for him."

"Oh really? Which one is he?"

"We call him M&M. That stands for Marriage Minded. He just needs to find the right girl and it's wedding bells for him."

Game over. White Spandex's eyes, in their nest of mascara, brightened. She backed off and took another chair, across the table. At her next eager question, Nelly put her hand to her ear in the classic deaf-lady manner, and the girl turned away. Being old sometimes had its advantages.

"Grans?" Melissa stood behind her, hands on hips, green eyes flaring.

"There you are! Just look at these seats I got for us. We'll have the best view in the whole—"

"A bachelor auction, Grans? Have you lost your mind?"

"Now Melissa, that's not a nice thing to say to an old lady." Nelly sniffed, looking, she hoped, deeply wounded.

"Playing the age card. You should be ashamed."

"Well, I'm not. It's my birthday and you have to do what I want. This is what I want. Now sit down." She tugged on her granddaughter's slim wrist, but Melissa didn't budge.

"I left work early to celebrate your birthday. Which means Ella Joy is going to write her own copy for the *Six O'Clock News*, and you know what happened last time." Nelly remembered. Three slander lawsuits had resulted from the anchorwoman's aversion to the word "alleged." "So the least you can do is explain to me *why* you wanted to come here for your birthday."

Nelly sighed. If Melissa wanted to be difficult, she'd have to play dirty. "I hate to point it out, but at my age, this could be my *last* birthday . . ."

"Oh geez, Grans."

Worked every time.

Melissa picked up Nelly's purse and sat gingerly in its place. "I know this is one of your crazy plans to butt in on my love life . . ."

"Oh, relax. Just try to enjoy yourself. You're too serious."

Nelly smiled at her lovely granddaughter. Melissa had forest-green eyes, deep chocolate hair that curled tenderly around her face, and, when she chose, a radiant smile. In this crowd, Melissa looked like a woodland violet in a field of flashy dahlias. Why should a beautiful, sweet, intelligent darling like her granddaughter have any problem finding the right man? Because—she didn't know what to look for. She went for the artsy type, graduate students and wannabe film directors, the kind of man more interested in finishing his thousand-page novel than in knowing how to treat a woman.

Nelly didn't want one more pair of wire-rimmed glasses showing up on their doorstep.

No, what Melissa needed was a prime, red-blooded, testosterone-loaded man. Someone like Nelly's dear departed Leon. She could hear him even now. *You want some sugar? Come on up here and I'll give you a big old heapful.* That's when she'd jump eagerly into his lap. Oh, the times they'd had . . .

"Look, they're starting!" Across the table, White Spandex adjusted her top and leaned forward. Revved-up hip-hop music blasted through the ballroom and a buzz of excitement shot through the crowd.

The auctioneer, a blonde with a high-voltage smile, strode to the podium and tapped on the microphone. *"Ladies, are you ready to meet the man of your dreams?"* The roar of whoops and cheers was so loud it made the silverware rattle on the tables. "Let's thank all the gentlemen who have agreed to participate tonight, and don't forget, all the proceeds go to the Widows and Orphans Fund, so don't be afraid to bid high if you see something you like! And I guarantee you will. They're all single, they're all sensational, and they're all sexy as heck! If you make the winning bid, not only will you get a romantic evening alone with your man, but if you bid on a fireman, you'll get an added bonus—a home-cooked dinner at the fire station! And let me tell you, some of these boys can cook. So let's get to it!"

The auctioneer quickly went over the instructions. There wasn't much to them. Bidders were supposed to raise their numbered paddles, shaped like fire engines, and yell out an amount. The crowd looked ready to rumble. Melissa, slouched in her chair, looked ready to disappear under the table. Nelly wanted to poke her.

"Drum roll, please!" shouted the woman. "Give a big hand to our first brave bachelor, his name is Dave, he's one of the guys over at Porter Ranch Fire Station 6 . . ." Dave from Porter Ranch, eyes twinkling, strode out onto the stage in jeans and a tight SGFD T-shirt. *Oh my!* Nelly felt faint as he began gyrating to the hopped-up electronic beat of a remixed "Light My Fire." Screams of approval rolled through the room like a fireball. He winked at the crowd, flexed his biceps, and turned to show off his muscular butt. Nelly gripped the table. The sheer energy in the room was overwhelming. Melissa, whose head could now barely be seen over the edge of the table, had a look of horror on her face.

"Bidding starts at one hundred dollars for a date with Dave. Did I mention he ran the marathon last year? This year he's going for the Iron Man race. He's fit, he's strong, and he's looking for someone to give him a nice backrub at the end of the day. Anyone here want to rub Dave's back?"

White Spandex certainly did. "I do! I do! Two hundred!" Girls from all corners of the ballroom recklessly yelled out higher and higher amounts. Before long the bidding was at a thousand dollars, and White Spandex, crushed, sank down in her seat.

The auctioneer banged the gavel and shouted, "Sold, for fifteen hundred dollars!" Whoops and hollers filled the ballroom as the winner collapsed into the arms of her friends. Dave crooked his finger and the pink-faced young woman made her way to the stage, where he brought her hand up for a gallant kiss that made her hyperventilate.

"Lucky," said White Spandex enviously. "But where that skank got fifteen hundred dollars, I don't even want to know."

"Grans, this is insane." Nelly could barely hear Melissa over the buzz of excitement. "Bidding on a man like some prize bull at a cattle auction? It's ridiculous."

"Shhh." Nelly decided to ignore Melissa for the rest of the show. "Here comes the next one."

The beefcake parade of Southern California's finest continued. All those powerful arms, those firm, flexing buttocks, those rock-hard stomachs. What about Vince from LA County Fire and Rescue, six feet seven inches of glorious sinewy coiled strength? Or José from Moorpark PD, with his laughing eyes and dance moves straight out of a strip show?

By the time Number Five was called, Nelly was ready. She'd circled and double underlined Number Five on her program. His name was Ryan, twenty-seven years old, a firefighter at San Gabriel's Fire Station 1. He liked dogs, hiking, and old-fashioned courting. He had blue eyes and brown hair, stood six foot two, and weighed in at a muscular two hundred pounds. Number Five was perfect.

And he obviously knew it. He strolled onto the stage in what seemed like slow motion as the music shifted to a slow, sensuous beat. With lazy blue eyes, he looked the crowd over, and a slow smile spread across his perfect face. From his slight slouch to the thumbs hooked casually in his jeans pockets, everything about him looked relaxed, easy, unhurried. He didn't need to dance or swivel his hips to get attention. All he had to do was stand in just that particular way. One sky-blue eye drooped in a slight wink, and a sigh swept through the ballroom.

The auctioneer could barely be heard over the din. "Meet Ryan from the most famous fire station in the country! You've heard of the smoking hot Bachelor Firemen of San Gabriel, now's your chance to get up close and personal with one of them . . ."

Arms shot up, crazy amounts were shouted out, and still Number Five did no more than stand, head slightly cocked. Nelly had no idea what the auctioneer was jabbering about, but that didn't matter. Oh yes, she thought. *This is the one.* The bidding became even more frenzied, but Nelly bided her time.

"Two thousand four . . . two thousand five . . . do I hear two thousand six? Come on ladies, don't be shy . . . two thousand six in the back . . . how about two thousand seven?"

When no more hands went up, and the auctioneer was lifting the gavel, Nelly rose to her feet. "Three thousand dollars, cash!" she yelled, waving her purse in the air.

Across the table, she heard a choking sound as White Spandex, who'd given up at seven hundred, nearly swallowed an ice cube.

Onstage, Number Five's eyes, blue as cornflowers, blue as a June sky, slowly drifted to meet Nelly's. She could see, just for a moment, a shock shimmering under the calm surface of his gaze.

"Three thousand dollars, that could be a record! Anyone for three thousand and one?"

Nelly thought she saw Number Five's eyes dart around the room, looking for someone, anyone, to counter her bid.

"Going once, going twice . . ."

The gavel dropped and the shout of "Sold!" echoed through the hushed ballroom. As a huge cheer went up, the fireman's lazy lids drooped, and his chiseled lips curved. He gave Nelly the slightest nod of his handsome head, and then strolled off stage at a slow-moving pace that set hearts fluttering and pulses racing.

Nelly sank down in her chair and put a hand to her chest. White Spandex glared at her in outrage. "If that isn't the biggest waste! What are you going to do, make him rock your rocking chair? Play solitaire with you?"

Nelly could still feel the adrenaline racing through her. Despite her skipping heart and shaking hands, she hadn't felt this good in a long time. "No, dear, I plan to give him away. To the most deserving girl, of course. Someone polite and well-mannered." She looked over to share her triumph with Melissa. But Melissa's chair was empty. Her granddaughter had disappeared.

MELISSA PUSHED HER way through the ballroom, transformed into a kaleidoscope of screaming faces and raised arms. She loved her Grans, but enough was enough. She'd wait in the lobby. If Grans came out, hauling a fireman behind her like a side of beef, she'd politely tell the guy her grandmother was suffering from dementia. Did Nelly really think she needed to buy Melissa a man? Didn't a twenty-nine-year-old woman have the right to pick her own dates? Compatible, mentally stimulating men?

She'd almost reached the exit when an overenthusiastic bidder jumped up, sending her chair skidding into the aisle, right under Melissa's feet. Crash! As she landed flat on her face on the ballroom floor, everything went dim, as if someone had fooled with the lights.

"You okay there?"

When she craned her neck to look up, she saw a man's powerful body silhouetted against the light glowing from the lobby. She wondered dizzily if she'd gotten a concussion, because it looked as if the fireman from the poster had come to life. He reached his hand to her, exactly the way the fireman in the poster held his hose. She blinked. He was still there.

THE FIREMAN WHO LOVED ME   145

The man bent down and untangled the chair from her feet. He hauled her upright. She was still marveling at the effortlessness of the move when he spoke again. "Leaving already? There's twenty more guys to go."

Dizziness was replaced by mortification. "No! I'm not here, I mean, I am here, but it's not because of—" She stopped. Her brain was just not working right. Maybe it had gotten scrambled by her fall.

"You sure you're okay?"

He had unusual eyes, she noticed. Dark gray, like charcoal. With little specks of silver. Right now those eyes were examining her far too closely. One firm hand gripped her shoulder. She shrugged it off. "Yes. I'm fine. And believe me, the last thing I'd consider doing is going to a bachelor auction."

"I see."

"No, you don't see. It's a birthday present."

"Firemen make nice birthday presents."

Was he making fun of her? "No! They don't. I mean, I don't know if they do or not, it's not my birthday, and besides, I'm not into firemen. I like, you know, writers. Genius types. Sculptors." *Sculptors?* Where had that come from?

"I hear there's an auction of bachelor genius sculptors down the street." The man's grave eyes had a little twinkle in them. He stepped back. Even in jeans and an open-collared shirt, his physicality shone through. There was something quietly powerful about him, something intense and contained. Maybe mid-thirties. A head taller than she. His face was weathered, with deep lines around his mouth, and stubble on his jaw. And those extraordinary eyes. It occurred to her that he was the only man in the place, except for the ones onstage. Of course! The truth clicked. He was just waiting his turn on the meat market.

"Are you sure you're okay?" he asked again.

"Yes. Absolutely. I don't want to hold you up."

He frowned. "Hold me up?"

"I'm sure the girls here are just dying to bid on you. You'd better get on up there."

"Oh. Well, no hurry."

So he *was* one of the bachelors. She felt a weird thrill combined with disappointment. Bachelors were, by definition, single. But bachelors selling their wares onstage were, by definition, not her type.

"I don't understand how you can do it," she blurted out. "Don't you think it's a little embarrassing? Dancing around like a male stripper, flexing your muscles and showing off your pecs or your abs or your glutes or—" She broke off with a gulp. Mentioning muscles was a mistake, because now all she could see was the hard outline of his chest under his shirt.

The man shrugged those powerful shoulders, a gesture she found annoyingly distracting. "If it's so embarrassing, don't you think anyone who does it for charity deserves some credit?"

Score one for the stranger. She scrambled for a response. "What about the girl who bids for you? It's not like you're going to marry her. You'll take her out once and never see her again, right?"

"That's the most likely scenario."

"So you let her spend all that money for one date. How could it possibly be worth it?"

The man quirked one eyebrow in the most maddening way. "Don't knock it till you've tried it."

Oh, the arrogance of the man! Macho men like him always thought they were God's gift to women. Just then, another wave of delirious screams swept the ballroom. "Your fans are waiting. Better go!"

She pushed past him. Her shoulder brushed against his and a shocking tingle raced down her arm. It pissed her off. Didn't her arm know she wasn't attracted to guys like that? It had no business reacting to a full-of-himself, muscle-obsessed fireman.

This was exactly why she belonged with a nice poet or maybe a singer-songwriter. Guys like that didn't make her feel all jangly and off-balance.

She put the fireman out of her mind and settled into a quiet corner of the lobby with a newspaper to wait for her outrageous grandmother.

An Excerpt from

HOT FOR FIREMAN

RYAN BLAKE NEEDED a drink. Preferably somewhere no one would recognize him. Finding such a spot in the sun-blasted town of San Gabriel on a summer afternoon didn't come easy. The town had quaint little crafts shops up the wazoo, but so far he hadn't spotted a single gritty, anonymous hellhole where he could prepare himself for his meeting with Captain Harry Brody.

Right on cue, he passed Fire Station 1, home of the famous Bachelor Firemen of San Gabriel and legendary for the heroics of its captain and crew. Time was, he'd been on the front lines of those life-saving, death-defying deeds.

He slowed his pickup truck and willed himself to turn into the parking lot, drink or no drink. Lord knew, his Chevy had made the turn so many times it could probably do it without him. But this time, it drove straight past the squat brick building with the cheerful red geraniums planted out front.

Face it, Ryan wasn't ready for his appointment with Captain Brody yet. Wasn't ready to beg for his job back. He needed a goddamn drink first.

A green and white Starbucks sign caught his eye. Several cuties in sundresses gathered around the outdoor tables like hummingbirds around a feeder. In olden days he would have strolled right in and spent the rest of the afternoon flirting with one—or all—of them.

But unless Starbucks had started adding tequila to their iced mocha lattes, the girls would have to get along with him.

He scanned the street ahead with its Spanish-style stucco office buildings and parched palm trees. Too bad he'd never been much of a drinker. He had no idea where to find the kind of drink-yourself-stupid-on-a-Wednesday-afternoon, out-of-the-way, loserville place he needed right now.

And then, as if the word "loserville" had conjured it out of his imagination, the sign for the Hair of the Dog appeared on the left side of the street. Towns in the sunny California suburban desert didn't have dark back alleys. But the Hair of the Dog did its best to inhabit one. Located on a corner, it seemed to cringe away from its only neighbor, a shop called Milt and Myrna's Dry Cleaner's, whose name was spelled out on a marquee along with an inspirational saying, "The bigger the dream, the bigger the reward."

If the Hair of the Dog had a dream, it would probably be to wake up as a medieval tavern. Faced with weathered wood, it had black planks nailed at random angles across its front. Either someone had done a clever job making the Hair of the Dog look decrepit or it was about to collapse. It looked like the kind of place where old geezers spent their Social Security checks, the kind of place frat boys invaded when they felt like slumming, and pretty girls avoided like poison because merely walking in gave them wrinkles. The kind of place guaranteed to be serving alcohol at two in the afternoon.

Perfect.

Ryan pulled over and parked his Chevy as close as legal to a fire hydrant. Silly habit left over from his firefighting days, when he'd always wanted to be close to any potential action.

Time to get blotto.

When he pushed open the door, the dim light stopped him in his tracks. As did the hostile voice addressing him with an unfriendly "What do you want?"

"Tequila," answered Ryan. "The cheap stuff."

"I'm not the bartender, moron. I'm the bouncer."

Ryan's eyes adjusted enough to make out a slouchy, dark-haired guy about his age who looked too skinny to be a bouncer.

"This place needs a bouncer?" He surveyed the interior of the Hair of the Dog. Just as crappy as the outside promised. Everything was painted in shades of black ranging from soot to shoe polish, except for the booths, which seemed to be a formerly hunter-green color. Just as he'd expected, a motley collection of oldsters slumped on the bar stools. He squinted. Was that an oxygen tank? The old man attached to it gave him a snaggletoothed grin. He nodded back.

Yep, this place was perfect.

"My so-called job is to weed out the jerkwads," said the bouncer.

"Yeah? What's your name?"

The friendly question seemed to throw the dude off. "Doug." He added a menacing frown.

"Hey, Doug, nice to meet you. I'm Ryan." He shook the bouncer's hand before the guy knew what was coming. "You're doing a great job, keep up the good work. How 'bout I buy you a shot when you get off?" He breezed past Doug with the confidence of someone who'd been in too many fights to seek one out with someone who wouldn't even provide a satisfying brawling experience. If Ryan wanted a fight, he knew how to find one. Right now, he just wanted a drink.

The bouncer seemed to get the message. Ryan heard no more out of him as he made his way into the darkness up ahead.

Was this a bar or a haunted house? Maybe the men on the bar stools were ghosts still hanging around for a last call that never came. A couple of them certainly looked ghoulish enough, although the intensely unflattering light provided by the overhead fluorescents might be misleading. Maybe they were captains of industry enjoying the tail end of a three-martini lunch. Maybe the atmosphere added thirty years and several age-related illnesses.

A girl rose from behind the scuffed-wood bar, her head clearing it by barely a foot. She fixed snapping black eyes on him, nearly making him take a step back. What had he done? Why did everyone seem irritated that a customer had walked into their bar? The girl had big dark eyes, straight eyebrows like two ink marks, and tumbled hair pushed behind her ears. She would have been pretty if not for that frown. No, scratch that. She was plenty pretty just as she was.

He gave her the smile that had made so many women his eager laundry doers, tax preparers, and back massagers. Not to mention other parts of his anatomy.

She scowled even harder at him. And geez, was that a snarl? Maybe she was some kind of creature of the night, hanging out with the ghosts.

"Well? Are you going to order or just smile for the security camera we don't have?" Her throaty voice, though grouchy, set off a pleasant shiver at the base of his spine.

"Is that why you need a bouncer?"

"What?"

"Because you tell everyone off the street that you don't have a security camera?"

"Would you order? I don't have all day."

"Yes, I can tell this place keeps you busy."

Could her scowl get any deeper? Ryan cocked his head and scanned her face, amazed that he still wanted to look at her anyway. Why, he couldn't say. Stubborn-looking mouth, a nose that turned up at the tip, long eyelashes, flashing dark eyes that took up half her face. Small too, like those kittens who have no idea they're half the size of the dogs they try to beat up. Probably a few years younger than he, maybe mid-twenties.

She shrugged and turned away.

"Shot of tequila," he said quickly. Something told him this girl wouldn't mind blowing him off and refusing to take his order.

With a sidelong look that told him how close he'd cut it, she folded her arms and surveyed the bottles lined up on the wall behind the bar. "We have Patrón Silver and Patrón Gold. The Gold's a little dusty."

All the bottles looked dusty to Ryan.

"What's inside's still good, right?"

"Got me. Any of you guys tried the Patrón?" She flung her question to the geezers at the end of the bar.

"Tried a glass back in '92, Saint Patrick's Day. Thought it said Patrick, not Patrón. Hit the spot."

The first hint of a smile brightened the girl's face. "You're the man, Sid."

"Any time, Katie, my love," crooned Sid.

"He has the memory of an elephant when it comes to his liquor," she told Ryan.

So that was her name. Katie. He liked it. A lot. It made her seem more human. He stared at her, fascinated by the change a whisper of a smile brought to her face. Good thing he caught it, because it disappeared in the next second.

"So? Silver or Gold?"

"Cheap," he said.

"Excellent choice." She gave him a sarcastic look and reached for the bottle of Patrón Silver. Up she stretched, high on her tiptoes, higher and higher. Ryan held his breath as her black top inched its way up, up, until it pulled away from the waistband of her jeans, revealing a sliver of gracefully curving, ghostly white flesh. It bugged him that his mouth watered at the sight, that he wanted to run his tongue from the soft tip of her lower rib along the delicious slope that led to her hipbone. This girl had serious friendliness issues.

But she was kind of hot, in her own particular way.

The view slammed shut as her heels hit the floor and she yanked down her top. She plopped a shot glass onto the bar and sloshed golden liquid into it. "That'll be four dollars."

"Can't I run a tab?"

"No tabs at the Dog." The old man with the oxygen tank cackled. "Case you croak before you finish your drink."

Katie smirked, even though Ryan could tell she was trying hard not to smile. "It's the policy of the Hair of the Dog to request payment with each drink. If you have a problem with that, you're free to go down the street to T.G.I. Friday's. They have that super-fun trivia game there."

She wasn't going to get rid of him that easily. "It's Wednesday," he said, pulling out a fiver along with his smile. "Wouldn't be right."

She snickered. Then looked so annoyed with herself that she turned away and headed for the cluster of men at the other end of the bar. He watched her every step of the way. Each line of her body radiated energy. She didn't walk in the flirty way he was used to. He'd watched many a girl sway her hips back and forth on her way to the ladies' room during a date. He always looked forward to the moment a girl would excuse herself and give him a show, a tempting promise of what was to come later on.

Not this girl. She had a direct and to-the-point stride, and was either unaware of her sexiness or in deliberate denial. Her odd choice of clothing—long-sleeved black top on a hot day—could go either way.

He tossed back his tequila. As the liquor entered his system, the dingy room acquired a lovely, blurry sheen. Just what the doctor ordered. And the doctor would definitely recommend another dose. He tapped the glass on the scuffed wood of the counter. Katie glanced down the length of the bar at him, pinning him with a look of disgust. "You aren't planning to get drunk, are you?"

"Do you interrogate all your customers about their future plans?"

"Only the troublemakers." She graced the geezer brigade with a glowing smile and headed back his way. For one moment, Ryan wished he'd brought his grandfather. Maybe this girl had a thing for older men.

"What makes you think I'm a troublemaker?" He motioned for her to refill his glass. "I'm all about peace and harmony. Kumbaya, my friend, kumbaya."

She looked revolted.

"We have more in common than what keeps us apart," he added wisely, after downing the second shot. He'd always loved a good affirmation, especially with a buzz on.

"You can stop now."

Aha. He'd found a sore spot.

"A hand offered in friendship opens more doors than a fist raised in anger. You catch more flies with sugar than vinegar." Okay, that last one wasn't an affirmation, but he threw it in for free.

"Do you want me to kick you out of here?"

"Make friends with your anger."

"Doug!" she called to the bouncer.

Ryan laughed. "You're cute as a button when you're mad."

"I'm not cute. And I'm not a damn button. Doug!"

But Doug didn't answer. Scuffling sounds came from the front door. Ryan turned on his bar stool, which wobbled a bit. Doug must be outside, because his bouncer stool was empty. Something or someone banged against the front door.

"Uh-oh." Katie didn't sound irritated anymore. A quick look in her direction gave him a glimpse of dark eyes round with alarm.

"Sounds like your bouncer's getting a chance to earn his pay."

"Bouncer." She snorted. "Doug doesn't even know how to throw a punch. I gave him the job because he can't tend bar. He's no good with people."

Maybe it was the tequila talking, but Ryan found so many aspects of that statement hilarious that he laughed out loud.

"What's so funny?"

"Oh, I don't know. A bouncer who can't fight? Or the fact that apparently you're the one who's good with people?"

The Glare reappeared. This time Ryan was prepared. It even felt warm and fuzzy to him. Must be the tequila.

"Never fear." He took the bottle, poured himself a shot, downed it, then stood up. "Sir Ryan to the rescue."

"What? No, that's ridiculous. Sit back down. Seriously."

But Ryan was three Patrón shots past listening. Whether she wanted it or not, she was getting a goddamn act of derring-do. Or should that be derring doo-doo, considering where they were?

He chuckled. Yep, definitely the tequila. Not to mention the anticipation of a good knuckle-buster. He'd sworn off fighting as part of his effort to rehabilitate himself and get back on the force, but when circumstances demanded it . . .

He flexed his fists and opened the door. Doug fell into him. Ryan caught him and ducked the hard punch that came next. While the man with the flying fists regained his balance, Ryan propped Doug against the wall, out of the line of fire. When he stood up, two men faced him. Two tough-looking dudes in black leather and black beard stubble.

"Man, am I glad to see you guys," Ryan told them with a big smile.

True, so true. Tequila was nice, but a throw down was even nicer.

He braced himself. The second man, who also happened to be the larger of the two, came after him first. Ryan lowered his head and caught him under the left arm. He lifted him up in the air and spun him around so his legs mowed down man number one, who stumbled to his knees. Ryan dumped the larger man on top of him. Painful groans ensued.

Ryan went into his fighting stance. It wouldn't be fair to kick the men while they were down. He wasn't fighting for survival here. This was strictly recreation. The two men scrambled to their feet. The larger one, who had so recently been twirling through the air, roared and charged him. The next few minutes passed in a blur of vicious punches and ducks and parries and all the tricks Ryan knew from his years as an impulsive hothead.

God, it felt good. Even the punches he took hit the spot. He knew from experience he'd suffer the consequences later. But that's what ice was for. He'd recovered from plenty of brawls, with nothing worse than a slightly off-kilter nose. And, frankly, he was grateful for that one flaw in his looks. Without that, someone might think him nothing but a pretty boy.

"Hey, pretty boy," growled the large man.

That did it. No one called him that without paying the price. Time to stop playing with these guys. Ryan kicked into turbo drive.

A jab to the kidney. An uppercut to the jaw.

When he got serious in a fight, whether against a man or a fire, he saw things in quick flashes moments before they happened. As if he existed in a time warp a few seconds earlier than the rest of the world.

A head jerked backward. Bloody slobber slung through the air. A man fell to his knees. The other man slumped on top of him. A hand lifted in submission, then dropped limp to the floor.

When Ryan stopped moving and things returned to their regular pace, he stood panting over the two fallen bodies of the intruders. By their movements and the whimpers filling the air, he knew they were fine. Pissed as hell, but fine. He wouldn't want to meet them in a dark alley, but then again, San Gabriel didn't have any dark alleys.

He shook out his shoulders and arms. He had a cut on the middle knuckle of his right hand, and what felt like a massive bruise on the left side of his rib cage. Nothing too serious.

He glanced over at the bouncer, Doug. His eyes were half closed in pain and his arm seemed to be hanging kind of strange. Someone better get the guy some help.

"Call 911," he called to the bar. "I think his arm is broken."

"Already did," said Katie, so close he jumped. Christ, she was right behind him. She must have been with Doug. Then he saw the baseball bat in her hand and took an alarmed step back.

"What was that you were saying?" She stepped toward him with blazing eyes. "Right before you got my bar all bloody?" Another step forward. Was she really going to whack him with a bat? After all he'd done for her?

"Um . . . kumbaya?" he ventured, hands in the air. "My friend. Kumbaya?"

"Yes! That was it." She drew back the bat.

"Now, now, Katie" came a wheezing voice. "Put down the bat."

Never had Ryan been so glad to see an old man with an oxygen tank, especially one who moved that quickly across the floor. He took advantage of Katie's moment of inattention to pluck the bat from her hands.

She stomped her foot with a furious look. "I wasn't going to bonk you, but if I did, you'd deserve it."

He shook a finger at her. "Peace and harmony, my friend. Peace and harmony."

Too late, he realized he should have taken away her left foot along with the bat.

"Ow."

An Excerpt from

SEX AND THE SINGLE FIREMAN

REVENGE, DECIDED SABINA Jones, was a dish best served on the side of the road to the tune of a police siren.

It had all started with Sabina doing what she always did on Thanksgiving—hitting the road and blasting the radio to drown out the lack of a phone call from her mother. Thirteen years of no Thanksgiving calls, and it still bothered her. Even though she now had her life pretty much exactly how she wanted it, holidays were tough. When things got tough, Sabina, like any normal red-blooded American woman, turned up the volume.

In her metallic blue El Camino, at a red light in Reno, Nevada, she let the high-decibel sound of Kylie Minogue dynamite any stray regrets out of her head. She danced her fingers on the steering wheel and bopped her head, enjoying the desert-warm breeze from the half-open window.

So what if she had her own way to celebrate Thanksgiving? This was America. Land of the Free. If she wanted to spend Thanksgiving in Reno letting off steam, the founding fathers ought to cheer along and say, "You go, girl."

The honk of a car horn interrupted Kylie in mid "I will follow." She glanced to her left. In the lane next to her, a black-haired, black-eyed giant of a man in a black Jeep aimed a ferocious scowl her way. He pointed to the cell phone at his ear and then at her radio, then back and forth a few times.

"Excuse me?" Sabina said sweetly, though he had no chance of hearing her over the blaring radio. "If you think I'm going to turn my radio down so you can talk on your cell phone while driving, forget it. That's illegal, you know. Not to mention dangerous."

The man gave an impatient gesture. This time Sabina noticed that his eyebrows were also black, that they slashed across his face like marauding horsemen of the Apocalypse, that his eyes were actually one shade removed from black, with maybe a hint of midnight blue, and that his shoulders and chest were packed with muscle.

She rolled her window all the way down, pasted a charming smile on her face, and leaned out. With her window wide open, the noise from her radio had to be even louder. "Excuse me? I can't hear you."

He yelled, "Can you please turn that down!" in a deep, gravelly voice like that of a battlefield commander sending his troops into the line of fire.

Despite his use of the word "please," it was most definitely not a request. Sabina guessed that most people jumped to obey him. An air of authority clung to him like sexy aftershave. But she'd never responded well to orders off the job. At the station she didn't have a choice, but here in her own car, no one was going to boss her around, not even a gigantic, sexy stranger. She reached over and turned up the volume even higher.

"Is that better?" she yelled through her window, with the same sweet smile. With one part of her brain, she wondered how strict the Reno PD was about noise ordinances.

She couldn't hear his answer, but she could practically guarantee it included profanity.

For the first time this miserable Thanksgiving, her mood lifted. Her childhood holidays had always been spent fighting with her mother. In her absence she'd have to make do with bickering with the guy in the next car over. As someone who prided herself on never complaining, she'd much rather fight than feel sorry for herself.

It occurred to her that he might be talking to a family member. Some people had normal families and celebrated holidays in a normal fashion—or so she'd heard. She moved her hand toward the volume dial, ready to cave in and turn it down.

The man rolled his window all the way up, stuck one finger—a very particular finger—in one ear, and yelled into his phone.

Sabina snatched her hand away from the dial. If he yelled at his family like that, and had the nerve to give her the finger, he deserved no mercy. Besides, the light was about to change and she was going to make him eat her El Camino's dust.

She stared at the red light, tensing her body in anticipation. The light for the cars going the other direction had turned yellow. The cars were slowing for the stoplight, and the last Toyota still in the intersection had nearly passed through. She poised her foot over the accelerator.

Then something black and speedy caught the corner of her eye. The Jeep cruised through the intersection. The big jerk hadn't even waited for the light to change. It finally turned green when he was halfway through the intersection.

Indignant, she slammed her foot onto the accelerator. Her car surged into the intersection. He wasn't too far ahead . . . she could still catch him . . . pass him . . .

A flash in her rearview mirror made her yank her foot off the accelerator. A Reno PD cruiser passed her, lights flashing, siren blaring. It crowded close to the Jeep, which put on its right-turn signal and veered toward the curb. She slowed to let both vehicles pass in front of her. As the policeman pulled up behind the Jeep, she cruised past, offering the black-haired man her most sparkling smile.

In exchange, he sent her a look of pure black fire.

Sweet, sweet revenge.

Sabina's cell phone rang, flashing an unfamiliar number. For a wild moment, she wondered if it was the man in the Jeep, calling to yell at her again. Of course that was impossible, but who would be calling from a strange number? She'd already wished the crew at the firehouse Happy Thanksgiving. She'd already called Carly, her "Little Sister" from the Big Brothers Big Sisters program.

Was her mother finally calling, after thirteen missed Thanksgivings? Annabelle wasn't even in the U.S., according to the latest tabloid reports. But still, what if . . .

Her heart racing, she picked up the phone and held it to her ear. "Hello."

Clucking chicken noises greeted her. She let out a long breath. Of course it wasn't her mother. What had she been thinking?

"I can't talk right now, Anu. I'm in Reno."

"Yes, skipping Thanksgiving. That's precisely what I want to talk to you about."

"I'm not skipping it. I'm celebrating in my own way."

"I located a potential partner for you. A very obliging guest here at the restaurant. He's letting me use his phone so you can install his number in your contacts." Anu, who was from India, claimed pushy matchmaking was in her blood.

"Seriously. Can't talk." Especially about that.

"Very well. You go to your soulless casino filled with strangers, drink your pink gin fizzes and pretend you're celebrating Thanksgiving."

In the midst of rolling her eyes, Sabina spotted the police cruiser in her rearview mirror.

"Gotta go." She dropped the phone to the floorboards just as the police car passed her. The cop cruised past, turning blank sunglasses on her.

A sunny smile, a little wave, and the officer left her alone. A few moments later, the black Jeep caught up to her. The gigantic black-haired man looked straight ahead, either ignoring her or oblivious to her. For some reason she didn't like either of those possibilities. Or maybe she just wanted another fight.

She reached for her volume control and turned the radio up full blast. The man didn't react, other than to drum his fingers on his steering wheel. Fine. She rolled her window down to make even louder, knowing how ridiculously childish she was being.

Thanksgiving brought out the worst in her, she'd be the first to admit.

The corner of the man's mouth quivered. Good. She was getting to him. The sounds of Kylie filled the El Camino, high notes careening around the interior, bass line vibrating the steering wheel. Adding her own voice to the din, she sang along at the top of her lungs. She might as well be inside a jukebox, especially with that gaudy light flashing in the rearview mirror . . .

Oh *crap.*

ONE HUNDRED AND twenty dollars later, she pulled up in front of the Starlight Motel and Casino. Why couldn't she experience, just once, a peaceful Thanksgiving filled with love, harmony, and mushroom-walnut stuffing? Her mother had always dragged her to some producer's house where she'd be stuck with kids she didn't know, rich, spoiled, jealous kids who mocked her crazy red hair and baby fat. She'd always ended the evening in tears, with her mother scolding her. "This is what we do in this business, kiddo. Would it kill you to make a few friends? Those kids could be getting you work someday."

Her mother had gotten that part wrong. Sabina had found her own work, thank you very much. And it meant everything to her.

The setting sun beamed golden light directly into her eyes, mocking her with its cheerful glory. Thanksgiving always messed with her, always bit her in the ass. On a few Thanksgivings, she'd tried calling her mother, only to get the runaround from her assistant. But now Annabelle was in France and none of her numbers worked anymore.

Damn. Why hadn't she just signed up for the holiday shift at the station and spent the day putting out oven fires?

She grabbed her bag and marched through the double front doors, only to stop short, blocked by a giant figure looming in her path. Even though she couldn't see clearly in the dimmer light of the lobby, she knew exactly who it was. A shocking thrill went through her; she should have guessed the man in the Jeep would turn up again.

"Well, this is a lucky coincidence," the man said in a voice like tarred gravel. "The way I figure it, you owe me three hundred and sixty-eight dollars. Cash will be fine."

"Excuse me?" She peered up at him, his black hair and eyes coming quickly into focus. Her stomach fluttered at the sheer impact of his physical presence. He was absolutely huge, well over six feet tall, a column of hard muscle contained within jeans and a black T-shirt. "If you're referring to your well-deserved spanking from the Reno PD, don't even start. No one made you run that red light."

"Sorry, did you say something? I can barely hear you over the ringing in my ears."

Sabina lifted her chin. If he thought he could intimidate her, he didn't realize who he was dealing with. She worked with firefighters all day long, not one of them a pushover. "Maybe you should try not yelling at your family for a change."

"Excuse me?" He glowered down at her, looking mortally offended. "What the hell are you talking about?"

Realizing she'd probably crossed a line, Sabina scrambled to recover. "Anyway, you already got your revenge. They gave me a ticket too. We're square."

"I wouldn't have had to yell if you'd had the common decency to respond to a perfectly reasonable request."

Sabina felt her temperature rise. He wasn't making it easy to make peace with him. "Request? Something tells me you never make requests. Orders, sure. Requests, dream on."

"You think you know me?"

"Why should I want to know you when all you do is scowl and shout at me?"

"Shout?" He shook his head slowly, with a stupefied look. "They told me the people were different out here. I had no idea that meant insane."

Sabina tried to sidestep around him and end this crazy downward spiral of a conversation. "I wish the police gave tickets for rudeness, you'd have about three more by now."

He blocked her path again, so she found herself nose-to-chest with him. Sabina imagined him as a Scottish laird or a medieval warrior hacking at enemies on the battlefield. The man was fierce, but annoyingly attractive. He even smelled nice, like sunshine on leather seats.

"How about drowning out a man's first phone call with his son in two thousand miles? How's that for rudeness?"

He had a point. But a surge of resentment swamped her momentary pang of conscience. So some people *did* talk to their children on Thanksgiving. Normal people, irritatingly, aggravatingly, unreachably normal people. People who were not her or her mother.

"Fine," she snapped. "Here." She dug in her pocket and took out a handful of change. "We're at a casino, right? Play your cards right and you'll get your precious three hundred and sixty-eight dollars. Good luck."

She lifted one of his hands—so big and warm—and plopped her small pile of change into his palm. With the air of an offended duchess, she swept past him, deeply appreciating the way his black-stubbled jaw dropped open.

So maybe she'd been wrong before. Maybe revenge was a dish best served in a hotel lobby with a side of loose change.

About the Author

JENNIFER BERNARD is a graduate of Harvard and a former news promo producer. The child of academics, she confounded her family by preferring romance novels to . . . well, any other books. She left big-city life for true love in Alaska, where she now lives with her husband and stepdaughters. She's no stranger to book success, as she also writes erotic novellas under a naughty secret name not to be mentioned at family gatherings. Visit her on the Web at www.JenniferBernard.net.

Visit www.AuthorTracker.com for exclusive information on your favorite HarperCollins authors.

Give in to your impulses . . .
Read on for a sneak peek at seven brand-new
e-book original tales of romance
from Avon Books.
Available now wherever e-books are sold.

THREE SCHEMES AND A SCANDAL
By Maya Rodale

SKIES OF STEEL
THE ETHER CHRONICLES
By Zoë Archer

FURTHER CONFESSIONS OF A
SLIGHTLY NEUROTIC HITWOMAN
By JB Lynn

THE SECOND SEDUCTION
OF A LADY
By Miranda Neville

TO HELL AND BACK
A LEAGUE OF GUARDIANS NOVELLA
By Juliana Stone

MIDNIGHT IN YOUR ARMS
By Morgan Kelly

SEDUCED BY A PIRATE
By Eloisa James

An Excerpt from

THREE SCHEMES
AND A SCANDAL

by Maya Rodale

**Enter the Regency world of the Writing Girls
series in Maya Rodale's charming tale of a
scheming lady, a handsome second son, and
the trouble they get into when the perfect
scandal becomes an even more perfect match.**

Most young ladies spent their pin money on hats and hair
ribbons; Charlotte spent hers on bribery.

At precisely three o'clock, Charlotte sipped her lemonade
and watched as a footman dressed in royal blue livery approached James with the unfortunate news that something at
the folly needed his immediate attention.

James raked his fingers through his hair—she thought it
best described as the color of wheat at sunset on harvest day.

He scowled. It did nothing to diminish his good looks. Combined with that scar, it made him appear only more brooding, more dangerous, more rakish.

She hadn't seen him in an age . . . Not since George Coney's funeral.

Even though the memory brought on a wave of sadness and rage, Charlotte couldn't help it: she smiled broadly when James set off for the folly at a brisk walk. Her heart began to pound. The plan was in effect.

Just a few minutes later, the rest of the garden party gathered 'round Lord Hastings as he began an ambling tour of his gardens, including the vegetables, his collection of flowering shrubs, and a series of pea gravel paths that meandered through groves of trees and other landscaped "moments."

Charlotte and Harriet were to be found skulking toward the back of the group, studiously avoiding relatives—such as Charlotte's brother, Brandon, and his wife, Sophie, who had been watching Charlotte a little too closely for comfort ever since The Scheme That Had Gone Horribly Awry. Harriet's mother was deep in conversation with her bosom friend, Lady Newport.

A few steps ahead was Miss Swan Lucy Feathers herself. Today she was decked in a pale muslin gown and an enormous bonnet that had been decorated with what seemed to be a shrubbery. Upon closer inspection, it was a variety of fresh flowers and garden clippings. Even a little bird (fake, one hoped) had been nestled into the arrangement. Two wide, fawn-colored ribbons tied the millinery event to her head.

Charlotte felt another pang, and then—Lord above—she suffered *second thoughts*. First the swan bonnet, and now this!

James had once broken her heart horribly, but could he really marry someone with such atrocious taste in bonnets? And, if not, should the scheme progress?

"Lovely day for a garden party, is it not?" Harriet said brightly to Miss Swan Lucy.

"Oh, indeed it is a lovely day," Lucy replied. "Though it would be so much better if I weren't so vexed by these bonnet strings. This taffeta ribbon is just adorable, but immensely itchy against my skin."

"What a ghastly problem. Try loosening the strings?" Charlotte suggested. Her other thought she kept to herself: *Or remove the monstrous thing entirely.*

"It's a bit windy. I shan't wish it to blow away," Lucy said nervously. Indeed, the wind had picked up, bending the hat brim. On such a warm summer day as this, no one complained.

"A gentle summer breeze. The sun is glorious, though," Harriet replied.

"This breeze is threatening to send off my bonnet, and I shall freckle terribly without it in this sun. Alas!" Lucy cried, her fingers tugging at her bonnet strings.

"What is wrong with freckles?" Harriet asked. The correct answer was *nothing* since Harriet possessed a smattering of freckles across her nose and rosy cheeks.

"We should find you some shade," Charlotte declared. "Shouldn't we, Harriet?"

"Yes. Shade. Just the thing," Harriet echoed. She was frowning, probably in vexation over the comment about freckles. Charlotte thought there were worse things, such as being a feather-brain like Lucy.

Charlotte suffered another pang. She loathed second thoughts and generally avoided them. She reminded herself that while James had once been her favorite person in England, he had since become the sort of man who brooded endlessly and flirted heartlessly.

Never mind what he had done to George Coney . . .

An Excerpt from

SKIES OF STEEL

The Ether Chronicles

by Zoë Archer

In the world of The Ether Chronicles, the Mechanical War rages on, and appearances are almost always deceiving ... Read on for a glimpse of Zoë Archer's latest addition to this riveting series.

He *had* to be here. His airship, *Bielyi Voron*, had been spotted nearby. Through the judicious use of bribery, she had learned that he frequented this tavern. If he wasn't here, she would have to come up with a whole new plan, but that would take costly time. Every hour, every day that passed meant the danger only increased.

She walked past another room, then halted abruptly when she heard a deep voice inside the chamber speaking in

Russian. Cautiously, she peered around the doorway. A man sat in a booth against the far wall. The man she sought. Of that she had no doubt.

Captain Mikhail Mikhailovich Denisov. Rogue Man O' War.

Like most people, Daphne had heard of the Man O' Wars, but she'd never seen one in person. Not until this moment. Newspaper reports and even cinemagraphs could not fully do justice to this amalgam of man and machine. The telumium implants that all Man O' Wars possessed gave them incredible might and speed, and heightened senses. Those same implants also created a symbiotic relationship between Man O' Wars and their airships. They both captained and powered these airborne vessels. The implants fed off of and engendered the Man O' Wars' natural strength of will and courage.

Even standing at the far end of the room, Daphne felt Denisov's energy—invisible, silent waves of power that resonated in her very bones. As a scholar, she found the phenomenon fascinating. As a woman, she was . . . troubled.

Hard angles comprised his face: a boldly square jaw, high cheekbones, a decidedly Slavic nose. The slightly almond shape of his eyes revealed distant Tartar blood, while his curved, full mouth was all voluptuary, framed by a trimmed, dark goatee. An arresting face that spoke of a life fully lived. She would have looked twice at him under any circumstances, but it was his hair that truly made her gape.

He'd shaved most of his head to dark stubble, but down the center he'd let his hair grow longer, and it stood up in a dramatic crest, the tip colored crimson. Dimly, she remembered reading about the American Indians called Mohawks, who wore their hair in just such a fashion. Never before had she seen it on a non-Indian.

By rights, the style ought to look outlandish, or even ludicrous. Yet on Denisov, it was precisely right—dangerous, unexpected, and surprisingly alluring. Rings of graduated sizes ran along the edge of one ear, and a dagger-shaped pendant hung from the lobe of his other ear.

Though Denisov sat in a corner booth, his size was evident. His arms stretched out along the back of the booth, and he sprawled in a seemingly casual pose, his long legs sticking out from beneath the table. A small child could have fit inside each of his tall, buckled boots. He wore what must have been his Russian Imperial Aerial Navy long coat, but he'd torn off the sleeves, and the once-somber gray wool now sported a motley assortment of chains, medals, ribbons, and bits of clockwork. A deliberate show of defiance. His coat proclaimed: *I'm no longer under any government's control.*

If he wore a shirt beneath his coat, she couldn't tell. His arms were bare, save for a thick leather gauntlet adorned with more buckles on one wrist.

Despite her years of fieldwork in the world's faraway places, Daphne could confidently say Denisov was by far the most extraordinary-looking individual she'd ever seen. She barely noticed the two men sitting with him, all three of them laughing boisterously over something Denisov said.

His laugh stopped abruptly. He trained his quartz blue gaze right on her.

As if filled with ether, her heart immediately soared into her throat. She felt as though she'd been targeted by a predator. Nowhere to turn, nowhere to run.

ZOË ARCHER

I'm not here to run.

When he crooked his finger, motioning for her to come toward him, she fought her impulse to flee. Instead, she put one foot in front of the other, approaching his booth until she stood before him. Even with the table separating them, she didn't feel protected. One sweep of his thickly muscled arm could have tossed the heavy oak aside as if it were paper.

"Your search has ended, *zaika*." His voice was heavily accented, deep as a cavern. "Here I am."

An Excerpt from

FURTHER CONFESSIONS OF A SLIGHTLY NEUROTIC HITWOMAN

by JB Lynn

Knocking off a drug kingpin was the last thing on Maggie Lee's to-do list . . . Take three wacky aunts, two talking animals, one nervous bride, and an upcoming hit, and you've got the follow-up to JB Lynn's wickedly funny *Confessions of a Slightly Neurotic Hitwoman*.

"I see a disco ball in your future." Armani Vasquez, the closest thing I had to a friend at Insuring the Future, delivered this pronouncement right after she sprinkled a handful of candy corn into her Caesar salad.

Disgusted by her food combination, I pushed my own peanut butter and jelly sandwich away. "Really? A disco ball?"

If you'd told me a month ago that I'd be leaning over a table in the lunchroom, paying close attention to the bizarre premonitions of my half-crippled, wannabe-psychic coworker, I would have said you were crazy.

But I'd had one hell of a month.

First there had been the car accident. My sister Theresa and her husband, Dirk, were killed; my three-year-old niece, Katie, wound up in a coma; and I ended up with the ability to talk to animals. Trust me, I know exactly how crazy that sounds, but it's true . . . I think.

On top of everything else, I inadvertently found myself hurtling down a career path I never could have imagined.

I'm now a hitwoman for hire. Yes, I kill people for money . . . but just so you know, I don't go around killing just anyone. I've got standards. The two men I killed were bad men, very bad men.

Before I could press Armani for more details about the mysterious disco ball, another man I wanted to kill sauntered into my line of vision. I hate my job at Insuring the Future. I hate taking automobile claims from idiot drivers who have no business getting behind the wheel. But most of all I hate my boss, Harry. It's not the fact that he's a stickler for enforcing company policy or even that he always smells like week-old pepperoni. No, I hate him because Harry "likes" me. A lot. He's always looking over my shoulder (and peering down my shirt) and calling me into his office for one-on-one "motivational chats" to improve my performance.

I know what you're thinking. I should report his sexual harassment to human resources, or, if I deplore the idea of workplace conflict (and what self-respecting hitwoman wouldn't?), I should quit and find another job.

I was getting ready to do just that, report his lecherous ass and then quit (because I really do despise "helping" the general public), but then the accident happened. And then the paid assassin gig.

So now I need this crappy, unfulfilling, frustrating-as-hell clerical employment because it provides a cover for my second job. It's not like I can put HITWOMAN on my next tax return. Besides, if I didn't keep this job, my meddling aunts would wonder what the hell I'm doing with my life.

An Excerpt from

THE SECOND SEDUCTION
OF A LADY

by Miranda Neville

**Enter the thrilling, sexy world of Georgian
England in this splendid Miranda Neville
novella—and catch a glimpse of Caro, the
heroine of the upcoming *The Importance of
Being Wicked*, on sale December 2012.**

"Eleanor!" She looked up. He stepped forward to meet her
on the bridge. "Eleanor!" He should ask her how she was, why
she was there. But he didn't care why she was there. All he
wanted to do was take her into his arms and tease her stern
mouth into returning his kisses.

His outstretched arms were welcomed with a hearty
shove, and he landed on his back in cold water.

"What—"

She looked down at him, grim satisfaction on her elegant features. "I beg your pardon, Mr. Quinton, but you were in my way. I have things to attend to."

As he struggled upright in the thigh-deep water, she completed her crossing. Cold soaked through every garment, chilling his skin, his ardor, and his heart. "Wait! You are trespassing," he called, a surge of rage making him petty. He'd been wrong, yes, but his intentions had ultimately been honorable. She had sent him about his business with a cold rebuke. And returned all his letters unread.

"Oh? Is this your land?" she said with a haughty brow, knowing well that his home was over a hundred miles away, near Newmarket.

"Effectively, yes," he said, clambering up the bank. "I have control of the Townsend estate for another three weeks, until my ward reaches his majority."

"In that case," she replied, "I'll collect *my* charge and be off."

Ignoring the squelching in his boots, he reached for her again. In the bare second his wet hand rested on her lower arm, warm under his chilled fingers, longing flooded his veins. "Eleanor," he whispered.

"Get your wet hands off my gown." She shook him off.

"Won't you forgive me?"

Her grey eyes held his. He'd seen them bright with affection and wild with ecstasy. Now they contained polished steel.

"I think, Mr. Quinton, it would be better if we both forget that there is anything to forgive."

Max deliberately mistook her meaning. "Good," he said. She watched him unbutton his clammy, clinging waistcoat with the outrage of a dowager. Yet she'd seen him wearing even less. Or felt him, rather. It had been dark at the time.

The garment slid down his arms. "I'm ready to apologize again, but I'd like it even better if we could begin a new chapter. Can we start again? Please, Eleanor."

Eleanor watched Max Quinton drape his wet waistcoat over a branch, in fascinated disbelief that, meeting her after five years, he should be stripping off his clothes. She trusted he wouldn't be removing all of them. The entreaty in his voice affected her, but only for an instant. Giving him a dunking had blunted the edge of anger that his appearance provoked, that was all. Nothing else had changed.

"I made it clear in the past," she said coldly, "that our acquaintance was over. Forever. Should we meet again, which I trust won't be necessary, you may call me Miss Hardwick."

"Don't you think that's absurd, given what we once were to each other?"

She stepped farther away from this unpleasantly damp man. Never mind that his figure was displayed to advantage beneath clinging linen, fine enough to limn the contours of his chest and reveal an intriguing dark shadow descending to the waist. It was true that his thick, wavy hair looked quite good wet, but she no longer responded to the lilt of laughter in his deep voice. "Our past relationship was founded on falsehood and meant nothing. I never think of you, and I'd like to keep it that way. We meet as indifferent strangers."

A smile tugged on his lips. It was one of the first things she'd noticed about him, that hint of humor in an otherwise grave face. "Do you often push strangers into rivers?"

"You deserved it."

An Excerpt from

TO HELL AND BACK

A LEAGUE OF GUARDIANS NOVELLA

by *Juliana Stone*

**All Logan Winters wants is to be left alone with
the woman he loves. But fate isn't on his side . . .
Logan and Kira are back in the latest League
of Guardians novella from Juliana Stone.**

Priest knew he was in trouble about two seconds after they exited the bed-and-breakfast. Up ahead, just past the giant pumpkin display, stood a pack of blood demons. They'd donned their human guise, of course, but it did nothing to hide the menace they projected. A family of five gave them a wide berth as they traversed the sidewalk, and he watched as the mother hustled her children past.

Smart humans.

The damn things looked like a bunch of thugs—all of

them well over six feet in height, with thick necks, tree trunks for legs, and shoulders as wide as a Mack truck.

They were mean and strong, but dumb. Bottom feeders who kissed the asses of most of the underworld. He wondered who they called boss.

Normally, Priest wouldn't have blinked. As an immortal knight of the Templar, he was used to dealing with all sorts of otherworld scum. In fact, it had been a few months since he'd flexed his muscles and connected his fists with demon hide. Normally he looked forward to this kind of shit because life, such as it was, gave him only a few moments to feel truly alive. Making love to a hot-blooded woman did that. Waking up to the smell of fresh rain did that. Killing a bunch of punk-ass demons did that. He glanced to his side.

But normally he worked alone.

Casually he leaned his tall frame against the brick façade of the coffee shop to his right and kept Kira out of view. The woman didn't say anything—she didn't have to. Her pale features and large, exotic eyes couldn't hide her fear. But there was something else there, and it was that something else that was going to make all the difference in the world. Anger.

He reached his hand forward, as if to caress her cheek. All the while, his eyes scanned the immediate area looking for demons. To anyone glancing their way, they appeared to be a couple deeply involved in each other. Lovers.

Priest ignored both her flinch and her quick recovery as his gaze swept along the street behind him. His liege—the Seraphim Bill—hadn't told him much of this assignment, but he knew enough. He knew where Kira Dove had been.

The gray realm.

It was a place he was all too familiar with, and he had to give it to her, the little lady had spunk. Anyone who escaped purgatory in one piece was strong. He'd never met the hell-hound, Logan Winters, but his woman had guts.

His eyes hardened when he spied a second pack of blood demons hunkered down near the bed-and-breakfast they'd just left. When he felt the unmistakable shift in the air that spelled real trouble, his insides twisted.

Lilith's crew.

Just fucking great. His Harley was nowhere near where he needed the damn thing to be. He was surrounded by demons, in the middle of a large crowd of innocents and this little bit of woman had the very bowels of hell on her trail.

A new scent drifted up his nostrils. Lilith's pack hounds were here somewhere, and their human disguises would be hard to penetrate. Those guys were pros.

Priest straightened and dropped his hand from her cheek until he drew her delicate fist into his large palm. Damned if he was gonna let the queen bitch of hell get to Kira Dove. Strong white teeth flashed as he smiled and looked down at her.

"You ready to rock and roll?"

Huge eyes stared up at him, their dark depths hiding a hell of a lot more than pain and fear. There was strength there . . . determination, and—he smiled—a fuck-you attitude.

She nodded and then whispered, "Let's do this."

An Excerpt from

MIDNIGHT IN YOUR ARMS

by Morgan Kelly

**For fans of *Downton Abbey* and readers
of Jude Deveraux and Teresa Medeiros
comes the brand-new tale of a love
that crosses the boundaries of time . . .
from debut author Morgan Kelly.**

Laura collapsed on top of him with a weak moan that he
sucked from her lips as he withdrew and coiled himself
around her, face to face, his arm cradled along her spine. They
were both slick with sweat, drenched in the only substance
that quenched what it had ignited.

"One doesn't learn *that* in finishing school," he murmured
appreciatively into her ear, when he could speak. She giggled,
hiding her face in his shoulder.

"I suppose you think me utterly wanton?" she said. "Isn't that a word you use these days, to describe women like me?"

"There are no women like you," he said, tucking a damp curl behind her ear.

"Not here," she agreed, snuggling against him.

"Not anywhere," he said.

Laura smiled and pressed her lips to his chest. He ran his fingernails slowly up and down her back, and she nearly purred. He loved the way their skin stuck together, as though they were truly fusing into one person. His eyes grew heavy, and he blinked, afraid that if he fell asleep, she would simply disappear. He didn't know the rules. He didn't know if there were any. They seemed to be making them up as they went along.

"In this time," he said, "are you truly not yet born?"

"Not for years and years."

"Then how is it you can exist, here and now, with me?"

She looked up at him, her head arched against the pillow. "I really don't know, Alaric. I only know that I do, and that I have never felt more alive than when I'm with you."

"If you . . . stayed, here, with me, what would happen when you *are* born?"

Laura rolled onto her back, her leg still hooked around him and her body pressed alongside his. She cradled her head on her arm, the sinuous curve of her underarm upraised. Tiny beads of sweat pearled her collarbone, a necklace of her own making. "I don't know. But my time isn't a good one, Alaric. It's a dangerous time, when the whole world has been at war with itself. I've seen things I can't erase from my mind. People have done things that take away their humanity—and now they are expected to carry on like decent citizens."

"I know what war is," Alaric said.

"Not war like this," Laura said quietly. "We can never be the same, any of us. Being here with you makes me feel like none of that could ever happen."

"Maybe it won't," he said gently, running his palm over her sweet flesh.

"Oh, it will," she said. "And then it will happen again. Time isn't the only endless cycle."

An Excerpt from

SEDUCED BY A PIRATE

by Eloisa James

In Eloisa James's companion story to
***The Ugly Duchess*, Sir Griffin Barry, captain**
of the infamous pirate ship *The Poppy*, is back
in England to claim the wife he hasn't seen
since their wedding day . . . but this is one
treasure that will not be so easy to capture.

"You're married to a *pirate*?"

Phoebe Eleanor Barry—wife to Sir Griffin Barry, pirate—nearly smiled at the shocked expression on her friend Amelia Howell-Barth's face. But not quite. Not given the sharp pinch she felt in the general area of her chest. "His lordship has been engaged in that occupation for years, as I understand it."

"A pirate. A real, live pirate?" Amelia's teacup froze, half-way to her mouth. "That's so romantic!"

Phoebe had rejected that notion long ago. "Pirates walk people down the plank." She put her own teacup down so sharply that it clattered against the saucer.

Her friend's eyes grew round, and tea sloshed on the tablecloth as she set her cup down. "The *plank*? Your husband really—"

"By all accounts, pirates regularly send people to the briny deep, not to mention plundering jewels and the like."

Amelia swallowed, and Phoebe could tell that she was rapidly rethinking the romantic aspects of having a pirate within the immediate family. Amelia was a dear little matron, with a rosebud mouth and brown fly-away curls. Mr. Howell-Barth was an eminent goldsmith in Bath, and likely wouldn't permit Amelia to pay any more visits once he learned how Sir Griffin was amusing himself abroad.

"Mind you," Phoebe added, "we haven't spoken in years, but that is my understanding. His man of business offers me patent untruths."

"Such as?"

"The last time I saw him, he told me that Sir Griffin was exporting timber from the Americas."

Amelia brightened. "Perhaps he is! Mr. Howell-Barth told me just this morning that men shipping lumber from Canada are making a fortune. Why on earth do you think your husband is a pirate, if he hasn't told you so himself?"

"Several years ago, he wrote his father, who took it upon himself to inform me. I gather he is considered quite fearsome on the high seas."

"Goodness me, Phoebe. I thought your husband simply chose to live abroad."

"Well, he does choose it. Can you imagine the scandal if I had informed people that Sir Griffin was a pirate? I think the viscount rather expected that his son would die at sea."

"I suppose it could be worse," Amelia offered.

"How could it *possibly* be worse?"

"You could be married to a highwayman."

"Is there a significant difference?" Phoebe shrugged inelegantly. "Either way, I am married to a criminal who stands to be hanged. Hanged, Amelia. Or thrown into prison."

"His father will never allow that. You know how powerful the viscount is, Phoebe. There's talk that Lord Moncrieff might be awarded an earldom."

"Not after it is revealed that his son is a pirate."

"But Sir Griffin is a baronet in his own right! They don't hang people with titles."

"Yes, they do."

"Actually, I think they behead them."

Phoebe shuddered. "That's a terrible fate."

"Come to think of it, why is your husband a baronet, if his father is a viscount and still living?" Amelia asked, knitting her brow. Being a goldsmith's wife, she had never been schooled in the intricacies of this sort of thing.

"It's a courtesy title," Phoebe explained. "Viscount Moncrieff inherited the title of baronet as well as that of viscount, so his heir claims the title of baronet during the current viscount's life."

Amelia digested that. Then, "Mrs. Crimp would be mad with glee if she found out."

"She *will* be mad with glee," Phoebe said, nausea returning.

"What do you mean?"

"He's back," Phoebe said helplessly. "Oh, Amelia, he's back in England."